I0623263

ZPOC

THE BEGINNING

ALEX LAYBOURNE

SEVERED PRESS
HOBART TASMANIA

ZPOC

CHAPTER ONE

The skies showed signs of clearing; the heavy, low-level cloud finally looking to be on the verge of retreat.

After six straight days of grey, the cracks started to appear. Sunline breaking through reminding them all that, while the world had gone to shit, the sun still existed. The reality they knew was dead—much like those who hunted them now—but the world itself remained.

The dead may have risen, but that does not mean all hope is lost.

Henry Graham repeated this line to himself over and over as he lay in the self-constructed shelter.

It had been several weeks since the shit hit the fan and the first real cases broke the national media. He could not say for sure, because, well, time no longer had any meaning. There was day and night, survival or death. He knew which one he wanted; for him, and his family.

Henry gave a grunt, rubbing his calf in an attempt to force away the cramp that threatened to eat through the lower half of his leg. He checked his watch just as the silent alarm sent a pulse through his wrist.

Unable to ignore it any longer, he placed his weapon, a Remington 700 .308, to one side, and stretched his burning limb. While not a professional by any stretch of the imagination, Henry knew what he was doing. He understood what it took to survive. His entire adult life and a good portion of his adolescence were spent preparing for days like this.

Sure, he never truly believed it would be the undead who decided to rise up and end the world, but he always knew, deep down, that civilization was fragile.

It cost him two wives, but they just did not understand. His obsession was not dangerous; it was life-saving. That they couldn't see it was neither here nor there. Those relationships were things of the past, a past that was not only long since gone but belonged to a different world entirely. Henry wished the women no ill-will. He loved them both very much, to that day he still loved them. He strongly doubted either of them would have survived, especially Cheryl. The levels of naivety she managed to achieve never failed to astound Henry. Her good heart and simple, trusting view of the world, planted her firmly in the first-wave group of the dead.

Henry took a long sip of water. They had strict rations, but his shift was almost over, and he had plenty of water left in his canteen. Only mildly cool, it refreshed his spirit and brought his mind back to the present. Lingering on memories was a surefire way to get them killed.

He stared at his watch again. It was getting late; the others should have been back by now. Henry slid back into position and picked up his rifle, settling back down with his focus set on the tree line. He would give them as much time as they needed.

Taron and Hector left earlier that morning on a scouting mission through the woods. While the group invested their time and energy in creating their safe haven in the time before the world ended, they could never have factored in the power the undead could yield, or the overwhelming strength a moving group generated.

As a result, they agreed to run a daily check on their perimeter. The precautions they had taken were good but not designed to withstand the impact of a large group. Their daily sweeps ensured anything that got close enough was taken care of before it could form a congregation.

Even though it was still early days, the patterns had become clear. The dead showed no inclination to work together, but yet congregations of them formed without any rhyme or reason.

Henry spotted a group of fifty the week before while he was on the edge of town. They were just standing there in the street, gathered around a crossing like lost tourists. He remembered it because the power was still on, and the traffic light above their heads was stuck on red. Just blinking. He wondered if that had been what attracted them, but none showed any interest in it, so he quickly dismissed the notion.

The group had not lasted long, after a bunch of survivors tried to make a break for freedom. The scent of a fresh meal reignited their individual desires, and well, the kids never stood a chance. The stumbling, shuffling creatures were just like the monsters in the movies of old. They always caught up with you.

"That's the problem with the dead," Henry had told his son, James, who had joined him for the scouting trip. "They might be slow, but they don't stop. They just keep moving. Like one of those tsunamis, they just push and destroy."

Once again, he shook the image away. He needed to focus. They weren't playing games anymore.

With his sight set down the scope of his rifle, Henry waited. They would be back soon, then he could get back to his wife, his son. Despite the fact they were both hyper aware and well prepared for the new world, he did not like being separated from them. True strength was found in numbers, and between them, they each brought something to the table that kept them a fully functioning group.

Henry sensed the movement before he pinpointed its location. Only a slight rustle, but it was clear. Henry watched the spot, his eyes keen, his finger ready to squeeze the trigger the instant one of them came into view.

Killing the dead was a strange thing to experience. Those not too badly torn apart had not yet had the chance to rot. They still looked human, and while it was easy to distinguish between them, pulling the trigger still took an effort, a conscious moment of thought. Henry knew that needed to change.

When the dead rose, killing became a much simpler act. To hesitate, even for a moment, could be the difference between their living or dying.

The bushes rustled again, parting as the deer entered the cleared space around their shelter. The young doe was small, but she would provide enough meat to see them through for a while, not forgetting the rest of the body.

Nothing goes to waste in the apocalypse. They had that phrase posted on the wall of the shelter. A basic rule, besides rationing, was taking every safe opportunity to bolster your supplies.

Henry watched the animal. She stood perfectly still, studying the land, no doubt thankful to have found a patch not filled with the hungry jaws of the swarming dead. Henry knew he could take her out. A single pull of the trigger, a slight movement, given the sensitivity of the weapon, and it would be over. He also knew that it was not his prerogative right now. He had to watch for the others.

He adjusted his focus once more, directing his eyes back toward the area where he expected Hector and Taron to appear, but not before the arrow pierced the doe's upper thigh. The animal gave a shriek as it sank to the floor. The arrow had torn through the muscle, leaving the leg useless.

A second arrow followed; a hurried and loose shot, it gouged open the creature's flank before nestling into the trunk of a tree. The shot only served to heighten the pitch of the beast's screams.

"Goddammit," Henry cursed under his breath. Turning his rifle, he fired a quick shot, the weapon issuing a quiet whooshing sound as it launched the projectile. The doe's head exploded with a puff of red mist, silencing the agonized screams.

Henry was only distracted for a moment, but in that time their two shelter mates returned, bursting into the clearing at a run.

ZPOC

The first zombie came behind them, stumbling through the trees, a coil of razor wire wrapped around its leg. The wire was embedded in the former human's limb, and with each lumbering step it took, more and more skin was gouged away.

If the thing felt pain, it gave no outward sign of it. The creature just kept moving. Until the rifle round blew its rotting head apart. Puncturing it between the eyes, the round tore a grapefruit-sized hole in the creature's skull.

The dead man collapsed to his knees, arms outstretched as if somehow in his final moments, he beat the disease and was looking to give thanks for freeing him from his burden.

Inside the familiar territory of the compound, Hector and Taron stopped, looking back behind them. Taron held his crossbow up, and stared into the woods, while Hector pulled a hunting knife from the sheath on his belt, the ten-inch serrated blade glinting in the sun.

Inside the hide, Henry kept his focus on the trees, knowing that something else was coming.

The first head bobbed into view and Henry fired. The spray of mist was enough to tell him the zed was gone. Outside, Hector turned and moved away toward the deer where another dead man appeared, crawling through the bushes, his face a mess of blood from where he had been bitten. His left cheek had been removed, causing his eye to dangle from its socket like a ball on a piece of string.

It clawed at the carcass, tearing a deep gouge in the doe's flank. It lowered its mouth to the blood that flowed from the wound, lapping at it like a man emerging from the desert. Hector was fast and slid the blade through the zed's head, using his foot to push the creature away as he withdrew the blade.

With the immediate danger taken care of, the two men gave the signal, and Henry left the hide. While he wanted to understand what had happened, he had other business to take care of first.

With his gun slung over his back and his supply pack in one hand, he strode toward their main shelter and rapped on the door. Three heavy knocks and the door opened.

"Go easy on him. He was just trying to help," Vanessa Graham said to her husband, placing her hand on his chest.

"Honey, I'm not mad, but he needs to understand that we are not playing games anymore," Henry answered, his voice stern but calm.

"He's just a kid," she said for good measure.

"I know that, but the world has moved on, and there isn't a place for kids anymore. If he is going to take a shot at a deer, then he needs to make sure he doesn't miss, for a start, and to know when it's safe to take it." Henry hugged his wife, kissing the top of her head.

"He's in his bed," she said, hugging him back.

The shelter they had made was predominantly underground, buried within the hilltop. It had taken them years to get it designed and installed, let alone stocked. The shelter was tailor-made for the five of them, with enough room for two more if the two single men were willing to share their beds. While there were no individual rooms, the beds were separated into their own recesses in the wall, with a curtain that could be drawn, giving the illusion of privacy at least.

James lay on his belly on his bed, a comic open on his pillow. He flicked aimlessly through the pages, certainly not reading, or even recognizing the images crafted onto the page.

Henry knocked on the wall. "Hey, kiddo," he said, taking a deep breath.

"I thought I could take the shot, but ... but it moved just before I fired," James said without turning around.

"I know you meant well, but you need to realize there's a time and a place for hunting. That deer was not the priority, and now we wasted a bullet and lost the meat. One of the zeds came through the trees and took it," Henry explained, keeping his voice as calm and cool as ever.

A patient man, Henry had enjoyed a career as a psychologist before the world ended. He wrote a column for a national newspaper, not the agony aunt columns, but something far more substantial, both in terms of content and pay. His work regularly appeared in numerous magazines and scientific journals across the globe.

"I'm sorry, I won't do it again," James said, rolling over to face his dad. At eleven years old, James hovered on the edges of puberty and had already started showing signs of the battle that was to come. His moods could change, and his morose back-chat fueled style of interaction with his parents only showed signs of worsening. But, he was a good kid and understood the world around him. As good as anybody could be expected to, at least.

"No, don't say that. This world doesn't allow you to be apologetic, James. You make a decision and you move onward. It might be right, it might be wrong, but we do what we do, and the consequences are ours to bear. If you see a deer, I want you to think about taking the shot, and if it is safe, or if circumstances give you no choice, then I expect you to take it. Hunting, killing to survive is key now. Never forget that, all right?" Henry asked, holding out his hand for a high five.

James obliged, but when the others began to scream, their usual ritual was cut short before they could bump fists.

"Grab your bow, but stay back with your mother," Henry ordered as they ran toward the entrance.

A group of six zeds had made it through the perimeter and had infiltrated their camp. One already lay dead on the ground by the time Henry arrived at the fight. Its head had been split open by Hector's machete. The man had a range of bladed weapons he was immensely proud of and knew how to use with deadly effect.

Taron had engaged another, firing a crossbow shot that buried itself neatly between the post-human's eyes. A doctor in his previous life, Taron was quick, accurate, and deadly.

With two down, Henry made short work of the distracted zed he took out, evening the playing field. The post-human wore a suit, the expensive material tattered and torn, stained to a hardened crisp with blood. He was missing an arm, which certainly reduced its advantage in a fight, but Henry did not take any chances, stabbing with a quick striking motion. The blade went in and out of the creature's head, making a sharp, almost crisp sound.

Henry was away and after another one before the body hit the floor.

Out of the three remaining, two were women, a fact they had all learned was important. The females, as in a great many species, were by far the more aggressive. There was a strength and ferocity to them that the male post-humans just could not quite reach. Not that any of them would be complacent with the males, they were just as likely to rip an arm off or tear open a body, it was just that the women had that extra edge when it came down to it.

Taron had reasoned that biology supported the apparent fact. Women were predisposed to have access to inner strength reserves that men did not own. A pool touched on in life when giving birth or protecting the young.

It made sense to Henry also, but the discussion on the matter was kept short, for at the end of the day, male or female, all post-humans needed to be put down.

The first woman—a younger girl, who, judging by the way her figure still held a certain pertness, could not have been long out of her teens before she died—charged at Henry. She stumbled as she swung her arms in his direction, the large chunk of flesh torn from her inner thigh sending her wide on her approach. She swiped at him, her long fingers ending in nails that still had a nicely manicured finish to them. They had been sharpened down to a fine point. Henry had seen it before. In the final days of society, salons were offering the service, turning their clients' nails into deadly weapons. It didn't help worth a damn.

Henry took a step back, allowing the creature to come at him again. He studied her walk and struck just as she put weight on her mangled leg. She as good as fell onto his knife, her eyes going wide in perceived shock. She fell away, black blood oozing from the neat hole in her temple.

Henry turned and saw Taron and Hector each dispatch their zeds in hand-to-hand combat. One on one, the post-humans were manageable, providing you had room to work and kept your cool. They became truly dangerous in a group.

"Are you guys all right?" Henry asked, his body tingling with adrenaline. Part of him felt guilty for the rush he felt, but he also understood it was a natural reaction to the skirmish. From time to time, he still needed to remind himself that dead was dead, and zeds were what came next. There was no getting people back from it.

"All good here," Taron replied, checking himself quickly.

"Not a scratch on me," Hector answered, holding his arms out for all to see.

"Of course not, I keep telling you, not even the zeds would eat a lawyer. Your meat must taste like feet," Taron answered, smiling at Hector.

Hector rolled his eyes. "I can't help that I'm an expert at this shit. I've put in way more time in building up my skills than the rest of you," he answered.

To many, Hector was an asshole. To the group living in the shelter, he was still an asshole, but one they had known so long, that his cockiness and arrogance no longer really registered with them. If anything, they turned it around on him.

"Yeah, the rest of us were busy building this place up and stocking it with supplies. Remember that when rations start running low," Henry added, smiling at the pair.

"Whatever," Hector snarled. Turning, he stomped back toward the shelter.

"Oh, come on, man. Don't be like that," Taron called after him, trying to suppress the laugh building in his throat.

"Leave him be. It's probably his time of the month," Henry said, just loud enough for Hector to hear.

There had been a time when his attitude had caused friction among the group, but they had found the best way to deal with him was with humor. It would often darken his mood even more, but the overall impact seemed to expedite the entire process and bring him back around sooner.

"I don't think so. His lips weren't bleeding," Taron answered.

Both men opened their mouths and drew breath with the intention of laughing, but a frantic scream for help soon had them looking back toward the trees.

It turned out that danger was an even more effective tool than humor to bring Hector around.

"It came from the south," he said, pointing through the trees beyond the deer carcass and the dead zed that lay slumped over it.

"We need to check it out," Taron said, sheathing his knife and grabbing his crossbow. The M4 Tactical bow was a work of art. They had all been jealous when Taron revealed the weapon during one of their last monthly meetings before things went south. The red dot sight alone made it a very popular toy.

"Nah, wait it out. They're dead now, whoever they were," Hector said, squinting into the trees. He tensed as if he saw something but relaxed a moment later.

"You can't be sure of that," Henry said, looking over at Taron, hoping he would back him up.

"That wasn't the scream of a health hiker spotting a fucking bumblebee. That was the sound of imminent death," the lawyer answered, his no-nonsense attitude shining through. "Why waste our time chasing a dead girl when there are enough of the posties out here to keep us on our toes."

"Because they are people. There could be more of them out there. We can save people," Taron said.

"You're not in the OR now, Doc. You can't save people out here. It's every man for themselves. Besides, we've got it good here. We have supplies and space to live in semi-comfort." Hector turned to face Taron. The pair argued like an old married couple yet were always the first to pair up when it came time to patrol. Even back when they were still just building up for the possibility of a disaster, they worked best together.

"You can't be serious. We are talking about people. Survivors, like us. What right do we have to turn our back simply because we were prepared? I mean, good god, man, we were just playing until all of this came along," Taron said, dumbfounded at the cold, calculating way with which Hector spoke.

Another scream rang out. "Help me," the voice cried, the words distinguishable enough from the pain that surrounded them.

"We're going to check it out," Henry said, deciding for the group.

They left at a pace close to a jog, with Hector bringing up the rear. He was naturally slower than the others, given his short legs and stocky build. Far from fat, he would be described by most as simply being solid. A benefit of his Puerto Rican-Samoan heritage.

Once again, Vanessa and James stayed behind. Not because they were woman and child, but because it was their turn to guard the camp. Plus, they acted as a standby reserve should things go south, and they need a cavalry charge.

They had not moved far through the trees before they spotted the area of their perimeter defenses where the zed had pushed through the razor wire. The recent rainfall had softened the ground and its persistence had seen it work the foundations of the makeshift fence free from the mud.

They heard the steady, and now all-too-familiar slurping growls that told them a group of post-humans was ahead of them, feeding on a fresh kill.

The trees were dense in that part of the forest but not so much that you could not make a path through. The cool autumn saw the trees drop their leaves unseasonably early, and while the weather had stabilized since, the nudity of the forest increased their visibility considerably.

The forest floor sloped upward, forming as a gentle hill that gave way to a long, shallow incline into a small basin below. The higher ground served to their aid, as it hid them from the zeds' baseline view.

Once the feeding started, there was little that could distract them, other than the scent of another meal.

"I count four," Henry whispered, looking through the scope of his rifle.

"I only see one victim. You suppose the other got away?" Taron asked.

"Only one way to find out," Henry replied.

"You fools are out of your mind. We don't know these people from Adam," Hector protested but to no avail.

Taron raised his crossbow and took aim. The red sight setting on the back of the nearest zed's head. "This should get their attention," he said, moments before firing.

The arrow shot forward with a quiet whoosh, covering the ground between them in mere seconds, embedding itself in the skull of its target. The post-human died without making a sound, collapsing on top of the meal, much to the perceived annoyance of its hungry brothers.

Henry and Hector advanced down the hill, with Taron keeping back to cover them from a distance.

The three remaining posties turned at the first sound of their approach. Their pale skin, painted with the deep red of fresh blood, made them look more like a troupe of murderous clowns than the living dead.

Snarling and gargling, they announced their attack. Henry met his first one with a heavy swiping blow. Less skilled with a melee weapon than Hector, he relied on his strength and the simplicity of their opponents. His blade sliced open the zed's distended belly, expelling a belched rush of gaseous rot. The blast rushed over Henry's face and made him gag.

He reacted to the dead man's fetid release by burying the knife hilt-deep in the side of the post-human's head. It dropped to its knees, landing in the pile of cold, black offal that had spilled from its gaping belly.

Hector made short work of his post-human. The kid could not have been very far into his teens, certainly not old enough to drink in its previous life. Not that age was a factor anymore. Once they woke up, all posties had a strength that bordered on superhuman.

Still, the kid's skinny build and baggy pants, which Henry assumed were dropped close to its knees before it died, made its movements clumsy and predictable. Armed with a knife in each hand, Hector jabbed the creature once on each side, kidney shots, and that pushed it to its knees where it continued to snap and snarl like a crack whore desperate to suck a cock and earn her next rock.

Hector put the post-human kid out of its misery by slamming a blade through the top of its head. The creature fell away, and Hector immediately turned to advance on the third.

The woman, oversized in the gut and even more so in the bust, was a messy sight indeed. The right-hand side of her face was missing, stripped down to the bone. They could even see gouges in them, from where her whatever claimed her life had clearly gotten over-zealous with their bites. She also had deep wounds in her sides and across her chest.

Henry paused for a moment as he wondered about her final moments. It was clear she did not die peacefully; she knew exactly what was happening to her. He gave a sigh and drove his blade through her face and out the back of her head.

"She was mine," Hector said, sounding disappointed.

"We're not keeping score," Henry said, shocked.

"We've got to do something to pass the time," Hector said, smiling. It was a strange expression and reminded Henry that there was something not quite right with that man.

In all of their days prepping and preparing, the simulations they would run, and the supply checks they ran through, none of their scenarios involved the rising of the dead. Well, apart from one of their very first meetings. But that had been for shits and giggles. Yet, in all of them, Hector was the first to raise the issue of combat and taking lives. He hid it behind his role as weapons officer for their shelter, and always had an answer thought out and ready to use. A lawyer through and through.

"Guys, look," Taron said as he moved his way down the slope to meet the others.

He pointed to the side where a clear trail of blood could be seen leading up and over the other side of the depression.

"Let's take a look," Henry said before Hector had a chance to complain.

They heard Hector grumble, but he followed along with them.

The three men crested the rise and did not need to look hard to see the injured person. He was on his back, reverse crawling through the woods. His leg was broken, a fact made clear by the way the foot was twisted over ninety degrees to the position of the other leg. The long shard of bone poking through the man's mid-thigh merely served to accentuate the injury.

"Help me," the man screamed.

"Quiet, you fool," Hector snarled, scanning the trees. "He's going to be like a fucking flare for those things."

"He's scared and hurt. What do you expect?" Taron asked, moving off toward the man.

"I expect you to have some common fucking sense," Hector replied, once again following the two men, in spite of his protestations.

"Guys, watch for any zeds. I need to take a look at this. We can't move him without a stretcher or some kind of splint," Taron said, dropping to his knees.

"We can't help him, period," Hector growled, but took his blades and turned to watch the trees.

"Ignore him, he's a lawyer. They're all assholes," Taron said, eliciting a strained smile from the injured man. "Bite down on this. I need to clean your leg, and well, I won't lie to you, it's going to hurt."

Taron grabbed a leather strap out of his pack, folded it double and placed it in the man's mouth before he had a chance to say anything else.

Taron grabbed his water bottle and washed the bleeding limb. The man cried into the belt, his face turning a deep shade of red. Sweat poured from his face.

"Easy, easy," Taron whispered, as he poured more and more water onto the wound.

The man offered no response, but his face paled visibly, and his eyes rolled back into his head momentarily.

"Hurry up, I think we've got company coming," Henry said, switching from his knives to his rifle.

"I'm going as fast as I can. This is nasty," Taron said, understating the task he knew faced them. "Even if I clean this up, we need to make a splint and get him back to the shelter. I have more supplies out there." Taron swapped his water bottle for a pack of bandages.

"We've got company," Henry called, taking two quick shots to put down the first two zeds that emerged through the trees.

"Oh crap," Taron said.

"Let us worry about them, you just work on him," Henry said.

"No, I mean oh crap, look at this," Taron said, looking up at the others, and then beyond them at the approaching group of zeds.

Taron pulled up the man's shirt and showed them the bite mark on his side. The wound was not deep but did not change the fact that the man was going to die, or that Hector was right. They needed to leave him behind.

"Shit, we wasted time on a dead man," Hector snapped. "I told you."

"Hey, we tried. We did the right thing. We have bigger problems now," Henry said, pointing at the encroaching zeds. They easily numbered into the double digits, and moved like a flood, fleeing, rather than hunting. Their growls hung in the air like the rumble of a propeller aircraft flying low overhead.

"What are we going to do with him?" Taron asked, looking at the man who was staring at him with wide-eyed horror.

"This," Hector said, stabbing the man through the temple without as much as a pause for final words.

"Jesus Christ," Taron cried out in surprise.

He shot to his feet, realizing his mistake immediately when the post-human flood turned and headed their way.

"Shit, we need to get back to the shelter," Henry said, turning to retreat.

While they had been busy tending to the wounded man, the zed flood had surrounded them; closing like a spreading fire, they inadvertently encircled their newly discovered prey.

There was no room for them to head back the way they came. Instead, they needed to move through the forest and the open areas that lay beyond. The other option being to engage the group, which none of the trio felt any inclination to do. Being vastly outnumbered by a horde of the undead did not promote an optimistic feeling of survival.

Taron set off toward the closing gap, knowing that not only did they need to make it through, but do so without drawing any more unwanted attention to themselves. Henry followed, with Hector bringing up the rear, dragging the dead body with him.

"What are you doing?" Henry asked, watching as Taron increased the distance between them.

"Saving our asses," Hector said, his accent coming through stronger when he was stressed.

He dropped the body and pulled out his knife. With a quick, sure motion, he slit open the man's belly, spreading the incision until everything that belonged on the inside leaked through to the outside. The rush of warm blood and innards tainted the air with a heavy, coppery aroma.

"We need to talk about this later on," Henry said, worried by the ease with which Hector did what he did.

"Sure thing, but don't tell me it didn't work. Look," he answered, pointing to the zombie group that was closing in on them, the tantalizing aroma of fresh meat drawing them in.

"Just run," Henry said, unwilling to admit that Hector was right.

They hurried off in the direction Taron had moved. He was no longer in their direct line of sight.

They broke away from the main group of the undead and soon found themselves following a hiking trail. The forest was filled with them, each one conveniently marked with colored placards.

They caught up with Taron, who, having noticed their lack of presence, turned and set up a watch, taking out three post-humans that had been stumbling away from the rest of the group.

"What happened? We had a clear run!" Taron asked when the pair finally appeared from one of the trails.

"We baited them," Hector said. "Let's get back to the shelter."

"We can't go back that way. There are too many of them," Taron said. "I've never seen a group this size before. It's like a goddamned herd."

They pushed on, following one of the trails, away from the group. Even with the main body behind them, the number of strays they came across was more than they had seen in the previous weeks combined. More than they had seen since leaving the city.

"Do you guys smell that?" Taron asked as he pulled an arrow out of the head of a heavy built zed. He had carried on walking a few paces even after the arrow had penetrated its skull.

"Fire," Hector and Henry answered in un-choreographed unison.

They broke into a run, sprinting past the lone posties, the fear of an inferno overriding the danger of a few lone zeds.

"Honey, get inside, lock the place down and whatever you do, don't go outside," Henry spoke into the walkie-talkie as they stopped to rest just on the edge of the trees.

"They are already in the camp," Vanessa answered, her voice hushed. "Everything is secure, but you can't come back, not yet, there are too many of them."

"I know, we skirted around them. We're on the edge of the woods. There is a fire or something driving them this way. Just stay put, and stay safe," Henry answered, replacing the walkie-talkie as they moved off once more.

The smell of the fire grew stronger, carried on the light wind that picked up as the day drew on. Yet the complete absence of smoke or ash told them the fire was some distance away, for now, at least.

They emerged from the forest and into the sprawling farmland that dominated the landscape between the big cities and the mountains that lay behind them. In the distance, a billowing cloud of black smoke obscured the city skyline. It plumed into the air, its mass so great and heavy the orange flames at its base seemed almost inconsequential.

"That must be what is driving them away," Henry said as he stood staring at the blaze.

"Just imagine how many there could be if that blaze reaches the city limits," Taron said. "It would drive millions of them out, scattering them into the wind."

"That's why we left. The city is a dangerous place. Letting it burn would be for the best if you think about it. They are mindless and slow. The fire would get a good bunch of 'em," Hector answered, watching through a pair of binoculars he pulled from his pack.

"Not enough of them," Taron answered, his words cold.

"Ain't that the truth," Hector said, turning to face the doctor.

"It looks like it's the power station," Henry said, peering through Hector's binoculars.

"I wonder what sent it up?" Taron asked, squinting, his eyes as keen as his skills with a knife.

"Probably just a surge. There's nobody left to man them places. They'll start to pop like corn in a pan before long," Hector said, turning just as a zed stumbled through the trees. He sliced its face clean off with a single blow, stomping on the brain that fell from the open-faced cranium, grinding the jellied mass into the ground like a cigarette butt.

"Dude," Taron said, watching as Hector scraped his shoe clean on a downed branch nearby.

"Come on, we need to circle back and try to make it back to the camp," Henry said, holding his rifle before him. "Let's keep clear of the trees and head up the old Blackthorn trail. It'll take a few hours, but that will bring us to the side of camp, and behind this flowing herd."

"Lord willing," Taron added, casting a quick glance up to the heavens.

Hector gave an impatient tisk but said nothing. As far as he was concerned his faith died with the rest of the world.

The walk back to the camp took them along the edge of the forest until they reached the river. The tide was strong, and it didn't take long before the first zed appeared, bobbing in the water like a tin can. It snapped and snarled, only staying afloat because of the gasses building up in its gut.

The men crossed the river, using the covered footbridge, and moved into the woods on the far side. The trees consumed them once again, and with the sun setting, a sense of urgency settled in. Not quite fear; that would be reserved for full darkness.

"Keep quiet, and keep your eyes open," Taron said. "We don't want them to come crashing down on us."

The sound of the rushing river had a soothing effect, but also served as a distraction, the rush of its tide masking the growls of the undead, potentially until it was too late.

One bunch passed close by but showed no inclination to attack. They stumbled along in the direction they happened to be facing. The herd appeared to have broken up, which resulted in numerous splinter factions forming. The post-humans showed no visible signs of bonding or being linked, yet there could be no denying their communal spirit.

Hector raised his machete and moved to strike at a stumbling zed. Its body was bent at an unnatural angle, the spine broken. From what they could see in the dim light, it was missing an arm.

Taron reached out and put a hand on Hector's shoulder. He squeezed hard and shook his head. Hector resisted, but as the zed shuffled away, Hector relented and turned back to them. "He was an easy kill," Hector whispered.

"Maybe, but what about them?" Taron said, pointing ahead of them where a group of half a dozen snarling, leather-clad, heavily bearded post-humans clumsily ambled their way. Both their numbers and their bulk promised to provide an interesting engagement. The blood caked into their beards proof that the group were more than capable of winning a skirmish.

"Get down," Henry said as the zeds' directionless stumbles brought them too close for comfort.

The group scrambled behind some trees, and for the first time, each of them was completely alone. While they knew the others were close by, the realization that they were not physically there, was a sobering one.

Henry pressed his back against the tree, holding his hunting knife, a simple Cold Steel Leatherneck six-inch blade. His hand was pressed against his chest, ready for a quick strike if needed. He felt exposed and alone. Even though his friends were only a tree trunk away, he could have been the last man on Earth in that moment and not felt any lonelier.

Henry's heart hammered in his chest as he heard them shuffling closer and closer, their growls a continual static-like noise that would surely drive anybody mad should they be caught among it long enough.

He heard a twig snap as the shuffling reached the trees. He held his breath, resisting the nearly overwhelming urge to close his eyes. He had to move. Once they reached the other side of his tree, one look back, for whatever reason, and they would see him.

Henry looked up. The sky grew darker and darker. Before long, they would be traveling blind. He swallowed that portion of his fear away. *One problem at a time.*

Moving slowly, he circled around the trunk of his tree, taking small steps, careful not to lift his foot too far off the floor for fear of snapping a twig or creating some other sound that would alert them to his presence.

He felt a wave of relief wash over him when he realized not only had they walked by his location but also the trees that hid Hector and Taron.

They were not safe yet, however.

As the day robbed them of their sight, their other senses became keener. The rumble of the post-human masses grew around them. The woods were full, teeming with the undead.

"We need to get back to the shelter. We don't have the gear with us to camp, and I don't fancy our chances of just strolling around all night," Taron said as the three men stood together once more.

"Which way?" Hector asked, his voice showing the strains of the day.

While they had been working on the shelter for years, having found each other via online survivalist forums, they had not spent enough time mapping out the forest. They knew the trails and knew which way would lead them to what the fastest, but that was a different skill than finding your way through the trees under the cover of darkness.

"Well, we followed the trail to the river that's now to the southwest of us. The camp should be to the east or thereabouts. I guess about thirty or forty minutes if we keep a good pace and don't come across any more posties," Taron answered, almost without pausing for thought.

"Why am I not surprised you know all that," Hector said, his gruff exterior cracking in the prolonged company of his two friends.

"I just have a natural sense of direction," Taron answered. "You know, the same way you have a natural sense of justice and … oh, wait, you don't."

The joke helped to relieve their stress levels a little, but silence soon fell among the group again as they set off through the trees.

When they first decided to set up a shelter, in the event of a world-ending crisis, they chose the spot in the forest for several reasons. One was the way the trees kept everything neatly secluded. Going off the trails would easily get someone lost unless they knew the area well enough.

The patch they had found was a natural clearing, which over the years they had thinned a little bit more. The shelter's primary entrance was on higher ground. They had the river within reach, which could be filtered and used for water, meaning their stores could be stretched even longer.

It took them several years to get it to the point where they first tried it out, spending a few days there, trapped with each other for company. The first couple of runs were awkward experiences, but they soon got into a rhythm and bonded with each other in ways regular friends in the world at that time rarely did.

Vanessa did not always join them, for James was a sickly child, and it was agreed by all that for the sake of the trials, it was not worth the risk of furthering whatever illness he had at the time.

While the main bulk of the initial post-human herd had moved through, there were enough hanging around to make their journey home a longer one than any had anticipated.

Hector all but walked into the arms of an overly affectionate older woman, her lipless face intent on kissing the inside of Hector's throat. She appeared from behind a tree, nearly jumping out like a child looking to scare her friends.

Henry reacted the quickest, not risking a strike with the knife, for fear of injuring his friend, but rather he shoved the amorous woman backward hard enough to create the distance needed for Taron to end her second attempt at life.

The blade silenced her growls with a slick wet sound, and while the darkness consumed her the moment she fell silent, they all heard the liquefied contents of her skull spill through the wound; dripping on the leaves like a leaking faucet.

The trio reached and crossed their perimeter defenses and felt a surge of relief at making it home in one piece. This was quashed the instant they saw the zeds milling around what equated to their front yard.

The remains of the doe had been spread around, the carcass stripped bare of the meat, while thick congealed lumps of its innards lay scattered in various stages of consumption.

The group did not hear the men approach, but the scent of fresh meat alerted them before any attack could happen.

"Today just isn't our day, is it?" Hector said as he pulled out two knives from his weapons belt.

"I'm fucking tired of this. I want some food and a good night of sleep," Henry snapped in a rare burst of temper.

Grabbing his rifle, he fired four times. The soft plop of the gun and the muted bursting of the heads he targeted provided little in the way of stress relief, but he could not deny feeling better. Taron disposed of the other two zeds, his crossbow an even quieter weapon than Henry's suppressed rifle.

"Hey, no fair." Hector jabbed Taron with his elbow.

"Quit it, man, not tonight. Jesus Christ," Henry said, storming off toward the shelter.

"What got him so wound up?" Hector asked, kicking the closest downed zed in the head with his boot.

"Well, I can think of a few things, but why don't we save that for the morning," Taron answered, slapping his buddy on the shoulder.

Hector held back for a while, watching as the others reached the shelter and hammered on the door. Looking around, he stared at the bodies on the floor. Crouching down, he pulled the two arrows out of the skulls of Taron's victims. "They still don't get it," he said to the corpse, whose lifeless eyes stared at him, the mouth pulled back into a snarl as if even in true death, the hunger still lingered.

With the arrows clutched in one hand, Hector rose and followed after the others. The woods were still alive with the growl of post-humans. In the distance, the fire still raged, and the city that lay beyond it was plunged into darkness.

Vanessa opened the door on her husband's signal, wiping her eyes dry on her shirt. She knew it would not help. Terror consumed her the moment the zeds swept into the camp. She understood why they had not gotten in contact; it was not safe. That did not stop her from being afraid. She spent the day weeping through fear of what would happen if Henry died. She imagined James growing up without a father, her without a husband. The grief had been paralyzing.

Taking a deep breath, gathering herself, she opened the door. The moment her eyes met her husband's, her resolve broke and the tears came back with a vengeance.

"I thought you were dead," she wept, embracing her husband, melting into his embrace.

"It was close at times," he answered, kissing his wife on the cheek. "Where's James, is he safe? Are you?"

"He's asleep. He was worried about you," Vanessa answered, looking down toward the bedroom area.

"I'll go wake up him and let him know I'm safe," Henry answered, giving his wife a final kiss before he walked away into the shelter.

Vanessa, watching him go, turned just as Taron appeared in the doorway. They smiled at each other. "Come here, you," Vanessa said, pulling the doctor into a deep hug. "Where's Hector?"

"Oh, he's alive, but just dragging behind. He enjoyed himself a little too much out there," Taron said, detecting a slight trace of disappointment on Vanessa's face.

It was no secret that Vanessa was not overly fond of Hector, but she understood the need to have him around. His callous approach to life completed their group. From the homesteader, the brains, and the surgeon, they had everything covered to live. Having the cold-hearted way of the lawyer meant they had what it took to survive.

CHAPTER TWO

The music thumped, the resonating bass turned up to full volume. The walls of the building shook, as too did the insides of everybody in attendance. They didn't care. There was nobody left to come and tell them to close it down.

With death waiting for them in the streets, the decision was made to party until the beer was gone, and then face the hard reality of the world.

The frat house was a teeming mass of bodies. Teenagers and twenty-somethings were pressed together, lost to the pull of the music, the drink, and the drugs.

People pushed their way through the rooms, and up the stairs. Combatting the airless, sweat-invoking temperatures by removing their clothes and losing their inhibitions. They had no reason to keep any of them.

While they partied and celebrated as if they had passed their finals and were ready to be let loose on the big wide world, there was a constant undertone of submission, which only served to heighten each individuals' desperation to cling to the good things in life. Or what passed for them, at that age.

The word had spread quickly. Not as quick as the virus, but nothing did. That was why it had won.

Students came from around the campus. What started as a party to celebrate the flu-like epidemic that had seen all lectures canceled and all deadlines indefinitely extended, soon changed into something much more.

The only rule was *bring your own beer*. It was fun, and as the dead started to rise, it was a distraction.

News of the party spread across campus, and people braved the new world in order to reach what was hotly contested as being either the last party of the old world or the first party of the new one.

Those who arrived armed with alcohol, music, food or any combination thereof were granted instant and permanent access to the celebrations. Those who came empty handed found the door closed.

It was fun at first but soon turned a shade darker when a young couple arrived as part of a group, who got entrance as part of a technicality, the majority of whom held a can of beer from a six pack.

After being refused entry, the two young girls stood in the street, their mood changing from stunned to angry. Their indignation at being rejected, for what was probably one of the first times in their good-looking lives was the ultimate downfall because the wandering dead had no qualms about welcoming the pair to their eternal party.

Their screams echoed above the thunder of the music, drawing cries and screams from those inside. The majority had never seen anything more graphic than a football injury or the sight of their girlfriend projectile vomiting, their lives traditionally sheltered up until that point. The sight of two young women being torn apart in a shower of dark blood and intestinal strands was too much for many of them. They shut the blinds and averted their eyes. They all knew the young screams would fall silent soon, and that there was no helping them.

For a while, the mood in the house changed after that event. What could only be described as an attempted coup rose up. However, given that the party was now under the control of the jocks, and nobody really wanted to risk being thrown out, it turned out to be a rather wimpy affair that petered out not long after it started. Three shots later, and the majority of people had forgotten all about it and were so shit-faced by the time the two young girls tried to gain entry again, that they did not recognize them anyway.

On the third day of partying, the drink was swapped out in favor of pot, a particularly unique brand of which was delivered by an overweight, bespectacled, and acne-fighting male, who within minutes became the hero of the hour and had his pick of any of the loose-legged ladies of the house. A card he quickly put to good use, if the sounds that emanated from one of the upper bedrooms was anything to go by.

The pot was fun, and everybody made sure to roll themselves at least one good smoke, but it did not come without peril. Three people tried to climb out of the bathroom window, making an escape with the promise of returning with food, mountains of food.

One man slipped as he was partway out of the small window; his trapped leg snapped before he fell. He landed in a heap, and the resultant screams drew all the attention that was needed to bring a good sized group of post-humans to the party. His two friends, who were stoned out of their minds at the time, thought they were imagining things. They still did, even after hungry mouths took the first bite. Several onlookers went as far as to laugh at the way the other man's blood spurted through the air.

As the days wore on, the scene in the house worsened. The weed disappeared, and the drink ran out. As sobriety hit, the full spectrum fear and terror ran through them all.

Panic set in, and people talked about the world outside the frat house in one of two ways. An evil dream that needed to be ignored until it went away, or a scenario that needed to be waited out. The unwavering faith in the military to resolve the situation would have been laughable had it not been such a life or death situation.

There were some, however, who knew that staying put would mean death. They knew it long before the pot burned out and the kegs dripped dry. They sequestered themselves upstairs, in one of the central bedrooms. The four friends, who had been relative strangers before things changed, sat back and resisted the temptation that came their way. They wanted no part in the power struggle playing out below them.

They did not know where they would be safe but knew that it was not the frat house.

***

"How long have they been going at it?" Julie asked, looking over her shoulder at the bare whitewashed wall.

"I don't know, but I'm getting jealous," Dwayne answered with a tired laugh.

In the next room over, the groans of passion had escalated to unbridled screams of pure delight, loud enough to drown out the squeak of the bedsprings and render the rhythmic thumping of the headboard against the wall to nothing more than a subtle bassline.

"It's got to be another couple. No way it's still the same guy," Jared said, sitting up on the bed.

"Speak for yourself," Samantha answered, giving them all a wink and a smile that instantly turned her angelic face into a picture of naughtiness.

"Oh, come on, nobody can fuck for that long," Dwayne said, subconsciously shifting his legs on the floor.

"Hell no, I can go for a good half hour, maybe forty-five minutes if he is good and makes me cum twice," Julie said, stating it so matter-of-fact that it shocked everybody to hear. Her petite frame, delicate china complexion, and deep auburn hair painted as being a quiet, studious type.

"With foreplay you mean, right?" Jared asked, the concern in his voice amusing for the women.

"No, I mean straight fucking. Not every time, but when I'm really feeling it," Julie answered, making herself blush as if only just realizing what she had admitted.

"Forty-five is good. My record is an hour and a half, but that was a real session, and I was kind of wasted at the time," Samantha said, once again her face a naughty delight to witness. Cute as a button, she was the giggly, flirty girl everybody loved, and who loved everybody in return. Hearing her talk of such acts made the two young men blush.

"Oh, well, that's impressive for sure," Dwayne said, unsure where to take the conversation from there.

"Hey, don't be like that. You're cute, and I'm sure you would be a wild ride," Samantha said, rubbing Dwayne on the arm.

His blush deepened, but he turned around on the bed to face the young woman. He smiled, as did she.

"Easy, tiger, that ain't happening. Not here, not in this house. While I enjoy sex as much as the next girl, I am not too fond of an audience," Samantha said, pointing at the other two. "So keep it zipped, and maybe we can talk about it later."

Her forwardness and the brazen manner with which she spoke about things had been a shock to them all, but in just a few days, they had formed a bond deeper than any they had known before. They sat and joked like old childhood friends. They swore and cursed, and at one point, somewhere on the second day, one of them even farted.

"I think they are done," Jared said, as the moans of pleasure subsided, a haunting weeping sound replacing them. The sort of noise that could only be conjured by a deep-seated regret.

"We should go check on her," Dwayne said, as they sat in silence, the tears making them feel more than a little bad about their mockery.

"You're right," Jared agreed, standing up from the bed.

The girls looked at them and stood without saying a word. The room they were in was a good size and had previously housed three frat brothers, none of whom had returned to it since the party began. It was untidy and smelled bad, but they had already come to think of it as their place. It was strange, but the idea of bringing someone else into their group seemed odd.

"Let me do the talking. I can understand what she's going through," Samantha said, looking at the two guys.

Both stood over six feet, and while Dwayne was ripped from years playing football, the main reason behind him being at the college in the first place, it was Jared who looked the tougher of the two. There was a strange manliness about him.

"I might need you guys to take care of the dude, or dudes, who are in there with her," Samantha added as an afterthought.

"Gotcha," they said, nodding at one another as if it were a normal Saturday night event for the pair.

Samantha unlocked the door, a precaution they had taken after the two young girls caused such a commotion. Turning the handle, she began to open it when suddenly Julie jumped onto her and pushed the door closed, slamming it hard enough to make the three jump backward half a step.

"What was that for?" Samantha snapped. "You almost took my fingers off."

"Just listen. Do you hear that?" Julie spoke as if she had not heard Samantha's comments.

"I don't hear anything," Dwayne said.

"Exactly, the music has stopped. It's quiet down there," Julie said, pausing to let the others catch up to where she was.

"Oh shit, you don't think–" Jared began, but he never got to finish his sentence because all hell broke loose on the floors below them.

The screaming began like a thunderous intro for a death metal song, while the crashing of furniture provided a pounding bassline. Panic descended in no time, and the sounds of death echoed up the stairs.

On the other side of the door, something crashed, causing the door to shudder in its frame.

"Help me, please, oh God, help," a young voice screamed, pounding her fists against the door.

"We need to help her," Dwayne said, reaching for the handle.

"No," Julie said again. "You can hear what's going on down there. Those things are in the house. We need to stay safe."

Julie stepped away from the door, her arms wrapping around her body. The color had drained from her cheeks and she stared at the door as if it were liable to come alive and bite them.

"We can't do that. People are out there, people we could save," Dwayne said.

"We let her in, take a look downstairs, and see what is happening. Those things are slow, we've all seen that," Sam said, looking from one to the other.

While they stood, the hammering on the door continued, incessant and frantic. The screams from below them had reached a crescendo, with the sounds of death and terror no longer distinguishable between the sexes.

"Fine, we take a quick look," Julie said, wilting under the gaze of her three friends.

"How do you want to do this?" Jared asked, looking at Dwayne.

"How about we open the door," Sam said, pushing the two men aside to take care of things herself. "Stand back. I'm opening the door."

The instructions seemed to reach through the panic on the other side, for the hammering on the door stopped. Moving slowly, Julie turned the handle and twisted the latch. She started to open the door, but something shoved against it from the other side with such force that it sent her sprawling to the floor.

In the instant that followed, the others froze, watching in near confusion as Sam landed in a heap. Lifting her head, she glanced back at the door, blood trickling from her lip as the woman from the room next door charged in.

She was nude except for a pink thong, which appeared to be wrapped around her left ankle. Blood covered her legs, flowing from a wound that, until that moment, the others had not seen.

"Help me, it burns. It burns so much," she wept, collapsing through the door, landing on all fours.

It was then that they all saw the source of the bleeding. The young girl's left butt cheek was nothing more than a bloody mush. Scraps of flesh hung like the frayed ends of an old sheet, while the richly colored muscle had been crudely ripped away with such force that the entire cheek had caved inward upon itself.

"Holy shit!" Jared cried out.

"Close the door," Julie shouted.

"It burns," the woman screamed as blood poured from her cheek, pooling onto the floor around her.

"Dude, the door," Sam screamed, echoing Julie's cry.

Dwayne stood, staring at the blood-soaked rear end, which continued to wiggle back and forth. Jared moved to close the door but saw it had popped a hinge during the woman's forceful entry. Despite his best efforts, he could not help but rip the door completely free as he rushed to close it.

"Shit," he said, as he stood holding the door.

"Just put it there for now," Dwayne said, taking the door and resting it against the frame. "Here, help me with this."

Together, the pair carried a flimsy chest of drawers and set it against the door, creating a casual barricade.

The room was filled with activity and suddenly seemed a lot smaller as everybody scrambled around the injured woman, who had stopped screaming and instead fallen into a trance-like murmur.

"Help me get her onto the bed," Sam said, taking charge.

Dwayne took hold of her feet, his grip slippery because of the blood, while Jared took her by the arms. Her body was limp as they lifted her from the floor.

"She's burning up," Dwayne said as he wiped his hands clean on the bedspread.

"She's dead," Jared said, from the other end of the bed.

Dwayne acted on instinct, his years of training in first aid—courtesy of his father's career as a paramedic—kicking in. He rolled the girl onto her side, placing her into the recovery position.

"She can't be dead, she's still moving," Dwayne said, as he repositioned her leg, trying to ignore the wet squelching sound her buttock made as he did.

Reaching out, Dwayne pressed his fore and middle fingers into the side of the young girl's throat, applying a gentle pressure as he searched for her pulse.

"She's burning up, but I don't feel a pulse." He watched the fingers on her hand curl and uncurl in slow, near-robotic movements.

It was Sam who took the opportunity to shriek then. She lashed out, swatting Dwayne's arm away just as the girl's jaw snapped shut, the teeth impacting with a hungry clack.

"Whoa!" Dwayne jumped backward, almost slipping on the blood-soaked floor.

"She's one of them," Jared said, as he sprang away from the bed, pulling Julie with him.

The room felt small before, when it had been the four of them. The addition of the bleeding girl had made it crowded. Now, with that same young girl dead, and thrashing around on the bed, the walls seemed to close in even more, to the point where they were all held in place, for there was nowhere to turn.

The girl stood from the bed but immediately stumbled. Off balance, she fell away from the group and into the wall. She snarled and scowled at them, her eyes clouded over with death. There was not a trace of humanity left in them.

"We need to get out of here," Sam said, raising her voice so the others could hear it above their own paralyzing fear.

Dwayne reacted first, shoving the chest of drawers away from the door. Jared moved behind him, grabbing for the freestanding door.

"Duck," he yelled to the two girls, who quickly obliged as he launched the door over their heads and into the path of the advancing post-human.

The door hit the girl, doubling her over, sending a burst of blood from her rear, showering the wall like a mistimed fart.

Nobody laughed, however, for they were all rushing out of the room and into the hall. The entire interaction had only taken minutes, yet it felt as if it had been a small lifetime. The adrenaline and the fear had blocked out everything, but now, as they stood in the relative safety of the hall, it all came flooding back. The sounds of panic and fighting below them, the hungry growls of the dead behind them.

"Look out," Sam cried, catching sight of something over her shoulder. She reacted before taking a second clarifying look, and ducked out of the way as the muscle-bound specimen of a jock swung his arms forward aiming to deliver a bear hug of death.

Julie screamed and slapped the post-human across the face, stepping backward as she did. Dwayne had his eyes on the stairs and the crowd of people trying to make their way up them. Sam saw them too, their blood-covered bodies giving away the truth, that their fight was already lost.

The naked jock gave a growl, his head turning to look at them all, torn between who it should eat first. Much like the woman, he was naked, his semi-erect cock hanging low and long against his leg, a strand of his spunk still dangling from the end like some sort of sexual lure. His muscular physique was topped off with a painfully traditional tribal tattoo that went over his shoulders and onto his arms.

Jared strode forward, balling his fist. He unloaded a shot into the fresh zed's face, shattering its nose and breaking its lips. The zed didn't feel it, however, recoiling a step, but not abandoning its attack. Throwing several more punches, and elbows, Jared turned the creature's face into a bloody mess before driving his knee up into the side of the zed's head. He heard the jaw shatter, and the body dropped to the floor. Yet, still, the creature did not stop. It crawled forward, the jaw hanging crooked on the lower half of its skull, snapping ineffectively.

"Fuck this," Jared said. Taking a short run-up, he punted the creature in the side of the head, the force twisting the bones until they snapped like a hand full of popping knuckles. "We need to move."

Jared turned to the others just as another visibly dead post-human emerged from the bedroom. Fully clothed, it was immediately clear that this intruder was the one responsible for the carnage, upstairs, at least.

Three blood-soaked bodies collapsed on the stairs, releasing the pressure that had been built, causing the remaining crowd to tumble to the floor. Clawed hands raked across flesh, tearing it like cloth. Blood spurted into the air, painting the walls and even the ceiling with its scarlet stain.

"We're trapped," Julie said, staring at the pile.

The bodies looked like a seething mass of flesh, bonded by blood. It was hard to tell the individuals apart. Their flesh was all part of one writhing whole. The slick sound of their ever wettening bodies sliding over one another turned the stomachs of the four friends on the property's upper floor.

As they stared, lost and held by a fresh wave of fear, the creature-mass before them ejaculated a shaken and terrified soul back into the world. Covered with blood, and rejected by death, the young man crawled away from the pile. Screaming hysterically, he seemed not to notice the others standing before him.

The man made no attempt to stand but crawled into the bedroom the four had just left, and into the waiting jaws of the young girl they had left there.

Dwayne moved after the man, shoving the tottering young zed aside with such force that her body flew through the air and onto the bed. She landed on her back, her body rolling back from the force of her fall, bringing her legs up above her head to hook beneath a book-laden shelf. Inadvertently trapping the girl, Dwayne grabbed the screaming boy from the floor.

"Shut up. Get a grip of yourself," Dwayne said to the man, shaking him in an attempt to silence the ear-piercing wail.

Dragging the man back into the hall, Dwayne let him go, half expecting him to collapse to the floor. To his surprise, he remained standing, and while his screams did not stop immediately, the heavy slap Sam delivered to the left-hand side of his face saw to it that they did cease.

"Get a grip, otherwise you'll die here," she snarled in a voice that demanded respect.

The man didn't respond but nodded and seemed to hold himself up straighter.

On the stairs, the mass of bodies still writhed, but the amount of blood and organs that slicked them made it impossible to tell who was who, or what was really going on.

"We can't stay up here," Julie said.

"There's no way down from this high up. We need to make it to the ground," Sam offered.

"I wonder. Come give me a hand," Jared said, nudging Dwayne with his elbow.

With Jared taking the lead, the two men approached the mass of bodies. He stood to one side of the stairs, and Dwayne the other. The larger man soon caught the gist of Jared's plan.

"On three," Jared said, raising his foot before he even began the count.

"Three," Dwayne said, not waiting for the full countdown.

The two men kicked out, pushing the pile of bodies with as much force as they could. Too gentle at first, their second and third attempts grew far bolder, and soon the bloody mass of flesh and innards was sent tumbling down the stairs, leaving a thick trail of blood behind. The ball of intertwined tissue bounced down three flights of stairs before coming to stop on the ground floor where it bounced once before exploding like a water balloon.

"Well, I didn't expect that to happen," Jared said as the two men peered over the second-floor railings, straight down to the bloody mess below them.

"Okay, the coast is clear, kind of … I think," Jared said, turning to the others. "Hurry."

The three didn't wait to ask or even think about what waited for them on the first floor. They needed to escape and knew that heading down was the only means to do so. Dwayne went first, with Sam moving behind him followed by Julie who led their blood-covered rescue, with Jared bringing up the rear. While he didn't say anything, Jared watched the man for any signs of injury.

They made it to the second floor but not without incident. Their bloody friend slipped on a strand of severed intestine and sent Julie, Sam, and Dwayne crashing down the final few steps along with him.

The three managed to keep their footing, but Dwayne collided with the wall hard enough to knock the wind out of him for a moment. The stranger landed in a heap and made no immediate attempt to get to his feet.

"I say we leave him behind," Jared said, drawing shocked looks from the others.

"You can't be serious?" Julie said, appalled at the thought.

"I'm deadly serious. I mean, listen to this place." Jared threw his arms out wide as he let the snarling and gurgling sounds of the house echo around them. "It sounds like this house is fucking digesting us as we stand here. We don't know this guy. We can't tell if he has been bitten or what. He is a risk, and not one we need to take right now."

"Dude, listen, you're right. You're one hundred percent right," Dwayne cut in, breathing hard as he rubbed his shoulder. "But we can't leave him. Not like this. We're not that far gone just yet."

Jared stared at Dwayne, not an intense stare down, or that of two alpha males butting heads, but a stare nonetheless. He took a breath and nodded. "Fine, help me get him up."

Together, the two men hauled the whimpering man to his feet. They dragged him across the hall and down the next flight of stairs to the ground floor.

The first floor of the house had a small corridor that led directly into the four bedrooms on the floor. The carnage told them all they needed to know and kept them moving forward. Nobody wanted to risk being the hero at the expense of not escaping the house of horrors.

The final staircase was a long, straight affair. The ground floor being unusually high-ceilinged when compared to the rest of the building. The devastation lay all around them. Bodies and parts lay spread over the floor, which looked to be a pool of gore. Not one spot spared a scarlet coating.

The door was to the left of the stairs, but it soon became evident that they would not be granted an easy escape, for a particularly portly post-human stood with his back to them, his head buried in the stomach of a particularly boisterous jock, Connor.

Connor had spent most of the party working the door and had been the main physical presence in the house when it came to keeping people out. His six-foot-six, near three-hundred-pound frame had played a pivotal part in his appointment. Not that it served him any favor in the end.

"Make it stop," he screamed the minute his gaze fell on the group coming down the stairs. "It burns. Make it stop, please."

The big man screamed and wept, despondent as the group quickly skirted around the stairs and away from the zed's direct line of sight.

All around them people groaned and cried out, arms reaching for the group like children desperate for a sip of water. One young girl sat against the wall, her belly torn open, and thick, purple strands of intestine cradled in her arms like a baby. She rocked them gently, her body trembling as she sat in shock. Her face was bedsheet-white and sheened with sweat. Her eyes stared forward, blind to what was going on. She had been lost to the agony of her demise.

A collection of fingers lay half chewed on the floor. Chomped on for a while, they had been spat to one side like pumpkin seeds. The goodness inside was gone, and the shell served no real purpose.

The echoing cry of the dead seemed to ring with a common tune. Burning. Those who had been unlucky enough to survive their wounds, screamed about the burning.

"We need to help them," Julie said, looking around her at the fifty or more bodies that had been torn through with such ease.

"They can't be helped," Jared replied. "They are either dead already, or they are going to turn into those things. We barely held back one, what are we going to do against fifty of them?"

Nobody answered him, but a growl came from behind the sofa, followed soon after by the snarling face of a hungry post-human. The creature swung its body their way, lurching forward as it stumbled over the floor strewn with human debris.

"We need to leave now," Sam said as Dwayne strode forward and swung a broken chair leg at the zed. The blow was heavy, the weapon snapping in two as it hit the creature's head, caving in the top of its skull. The wound created oozed a stream of sour smelling puss, which ran down the creature's face and into its snarling mouth.

"Through here. Hurry," a voice called out as a loud scraping sound rumbled through the house.

Turning, they saw a figure in the kitchen area, waving them closer. "Hurry."

Sprinting into the kitchen, with several zeds on their heels, the group found a host of other survivors. The scraping sound came again and they realized it was a heavy refrigerator unit being moved to block the door opening.

The small kitchen was a pigsty and had been even before the zeds made it into the house. Empty bottles, crushed cans, and dirty glasses lined every surface. Broken variants of the same lay on the floor, while the sink, which had been filled with ice at the start of things, was now a small pool of some foul-smelling substance they could only assume was vomit.

"That's disgusting," Julie said, bringing her hand to her mouth to try to hide her retching.

"Did you even see what was going on out there?" scoffed some yuppie in a fraternity jacket and a ridiculous baseball cap.

"What happened?" Samantha asked.

"How the hell am I supposed to know?" the same frat boy snapped in response.

"Hey, easy, we are all here together. She just means, how did they get inside? I thought you guys were, well, vetting people or whatever," Jared said, staring at the frat boy as if he had a serious problem with his presence.

"For beer, dude. Christ on a cross, if they had beer–"

"Or were really smoking hot," another voice interrupted, much to the frat boy's amusement.

"Yeah, if they had beer, or were really freaking hot, then that paid for admission. I mean, come on, it's a kegger, school's out forever!" The guy laughed and cheered, causing a round of hoots to echo around the room.

He stopped the instant Jared's head collided with his face. The blow shook the man and wobbled his legs. Blood streamed from the broken nose, painting the lower half of his face a deep crimson.

"What did you do that for, mate?" someone asked.

"You guys really don't get it, do you?" Jared said before the other frat boys in the room came to the aid of their stricken brethren.

Chaos erupted, with fists and feet flying in all directions. Jared fought like a man possessed and held his own for a long time. The numbers game was to his disadvantage however. Despite how many of the group he knocked to the floor, they just seemed to keep coming at him.

Two men grabbed his arms and pinned them behind his back while a third picked himself up off the floor and drove his fist into Jared's gut. Even with the two men holding him up, Jared was doubled over by the blow, the air driven from his lungs.

A knee to the side of the head sent him to the floor, which should have been the end of it, but the first frat boy stood up again, an evil smirk spread across his blood-stained face. Moving like a pack, they started putting the boot to Jared, stamping and kicking at him as he tried in vain to get back to his feet.

"Stop it."

"You're killing him."

"Jerry, Jerry, give it a rest."

"Get off him," a cacophony of voices cried out as the beating continued.

Dwayne moved toward the group, his ham-sized fists balled and ready to cause some damage, but he was hauled backward. Caught off guard, he stumbled as the blood-covered figure they had saved charged forward.

Diving into the group, he yelled and pushed, not striking but still managing to clear a space around helpless Jared.

"Quit it. What the fuck, guys?" It was only when the figure spoke they realized who it was beneath the gory disguise.

"Ian?" a young woman asked, pushing both Sam and Julie out of the way.

"Pack it in, everybody. We need to work together if we want to survive this." The blood-soaked frat boy roared.

Ian Spencer was the richest kid in the university. His family held long-standing connections through all levels of faculty and alumni. There were two different locations on campus that shared his name. There were even strong rumors he was related to the British Spencers and Lady Diana, but nobody ever dared ask.

"Shit, Ian, what happened to you, bro?" one of the frat boys asked.

"What the fuck do you think, Tank?" Ian snapped, clearly not in the mood for small talk. "These guys saved my life, they are solid, and you will leave them alone. Do you understand?"

For many years, Ian had been the popular kid in school because of his money. He was not the biggest, fastest, or the strongest. He was smart, and not that anybody would know it from his public persona, but hardworking, too.

"He fucking chinned me, the bastard. He got what he deserved," the bloodied-up man spoke.

"Well, you kind of had it coming. We all did." The remorse in Ian's words cut through the room.

"Bullshit. It was a party. Heck, it was your idea, man," said Tank, a big man with cold blue eyes and a mop of nearly white-blond hair.

"Yes, and I was wrong. Look at me, look at this place. We were wrong, and if we want to survive, then we have to work together," Ian said, reiterating his first statement.

"Fuck that. We are waiting in here for those things to leave," another of Jared's attackers spoke.

"Then you will die here." Sam took a chance at injecting herself into the conversation. "Do you want that?"

The man looked at Sam and smiled, tilting his head as he answered. "If I got to die with you by my side, baby, then why not."

Sam gave him a belittling laugh, walked forward and slapped him across the face, hard enough for her hand to go numb.

The ruckus threatened to kick off again before Dwayne interjected himself into proceedings. His sheer size turned the tide of the conversation just long enough for the temper flare to subside.

"We are getting out of here. You can come with us if you want, but we are not going to stand around waiting to be eaten," Sam spoke up, looking around the group rather than focusing on anybody in particular.

There were eight others in the kitchen, which when added to their four, made for a close quarter's discussion. Emotions hung rife, the atmosphere charged and balanced on a delicate edge.

"Dude, maybe she's right. I mean, look around, the party is kind of over," one from the group spoke, looking at Tank.

"There's safety in numbers, man," Ian added, trying hard to convince them to leave.

"We'd better arm ourselves because those things don't back down from a fight," Tank spoke, and while his words were defiant, he never took his eyes off Dwayne.

"That's a good idea," Julie said, speaking for the first time. "We've all seen the movies, we know how this works."

A few moments later, they were all armed with varying degrees of effectiveness. Knives had disappeared fast, with Tank insisting he needed two. The kitchen furniture had been ripped apart with chair legs becoming clubs with minimum effort. Others had turned to the broken bottles, holding the jagged things out before them like some sort of holy item.

"Are we ready?" Sam asked, as she once again found herself preparing to open a door to the unknown. She swallowed hard. They were not safe in the house. She knew that and accepted it, but what threw her off kilter was the knowledge that they would be in equal peril on the other side.

The increased space also meant an increased number of zeds, and that was something she was keen to avoid.

"Get on with it," Tank growled, clutching the knives in his white-knuckled fists. He had a strange, showboating smile on his face.

"That guy will die first," Jared leaned in close and whispered to Dwayne.

Jared had not spoken much since his beating but had dusted himself off, armed himself, and took center position immediately behind Sam.

The door opened and the cool air of the early morning rushed in, ushering with it the echo of the growling terror that was their world.

***

The fraternity house was located on the outskirts of the university campus, or technically speaking, off campus, for that ended on the other side of the road, out front. In turn, the university was nestled outside of the city, in a quiet and picturesque rural area.

The rear of the property gave way to an extended garden area, marked by a makeshift fence, but it all fed seamlessly into the sprawling fields and meadows that bordered the woods and eventually carried on through to the mountains.

As the group snuck out of the house, creeping like naughty teens sneaking out without alerting mom and dad, they looked around them, shocked that everything looked so normal. The garden was still there, overgrown and in need of some maintenance before the first barbecue parties started in the spring. The pool, which the frat house had paid for with the profits from their near legendary parties, still stood, uncovered and uninviting given the cold weather. The hot tub attached to it was not only steaming but occupied. The two figures sat arm-in-arm, and from a distance, appeared to be lost in a heavy lip-locking session.

"Hell yeah!" Tank slapped Ian on the back, pointing at the couple. He surprised them all with his calm and quiet tones.

"Grow up, you fool," Sam snarled at him. "They are going to get themselves killed."

"Maybe you're just jealous," Tank shot back, garnering a titter of flirtatious giggles from the women who had been part of those holed up in the kitchen. "You might not be so uptight if you got laid now and then."

Sam clenched her fists in an attempt to control herself, but the laughter that was being directed at her, in response to his cheap, schoolboy antics made her blood boil. She spun around to say something, but once again Ian interjected himself as a peacekeeper between the two groups.

"Cut it out, Tank. It's not funny, and now isn't the fucking time." Turning back to Sam, he gave her a shy smile, which she returned, feeling unusually awkward about doing so.

"The rest of the garden looks clear," Jared said as he and Dwayne returned to the group. Julie knew of their plans and had seen them wander off. The others, it appeared, were still oblivious to the danger around them.

"Great, so we are outside in the cold, sober, and well, lost. This sucks," one of the pretty young things in the new group said, her whiny voice an instant source of irritation.

"Then go back inside again," Jared snapped, standing up straight as one guy in a university football shirt moved in front of the girl.

Dwayne sensed the trouble and instantly put himself between the two men. He took hold of Jared and tried to laugh it off, but there was something in his eyes that gave Dwayne reason to pause. There was a fearlessness in them, not a cocky edge, but a cold one.

"Calm down, man, just let it drop. Like Ian said, we are in this together, so let's try to get along." Dwayne relaxed when he saw Jared's shoulders slouch, and the stiffness disappear from his jaw.

"But seriously," the other girl said, "what's the plan?"

For a few moments, nobody spoke. Half of the group was afraid to come up with a suggestion, some were lost and wanted nothing more than to move where they were told, and the others were still staring at the scene in the hot tub.

"I say we head back to the campus," Tank said, once again talking as if he were on some jock-fueled campaign trail. "There are enough buildings there and places to hide. People too. There's bound to be enough people there. We can hole up somewhere and wait for the cops to come through."

"Cops?" the jersey guy said, tilting his head in visible confusion.

"Cops, the army, anybody with guns," Tank replied, annoyed at having to offer clarification.

"No offense," Jared said, holding his hands up when all eyes turned to him, "but that plan sucks balls."

"Oh, really, shit-for-brains, then tell us, how are you going to save us?" Tank growled as a vein began to show on the side of his neck.

"We should head for the mountains. Right now, the key to all of this is survival. That means getting out of the city, away from the populace. The zeds won't necessarily come out that far, not straight away at least, and any that are there will be far less in number than around here." Jared outlined his plan as the others stood around him open-mouthed. "It seems as though you only get turned into one of them if they bite you. That means it's not airborne, yet, and isn't contagious, like the flu or anything like that, so we have a chance. The higher ground of the mountains offers us everything."

It took a few seconds for the words to fully sink through, and while Dwayne, Julie, and Sam were nodding their understanding, it was clear the second faction of their delicately constructed group held differed views.

"That's bullshit. The military won't sweep through the mountains looking for people. Heck no. We are going to the university, get some food, some sleep, and wait for them to come save our asses. I mean, come on, dude, this is America, not some backwater country in European or something," Tank snapped. "Our military is the best, and they will save us."

"Well, first of all, it's Europe, not European, meathead, and second, if you really believe that, then you are a prime example of everything that is wrong with this country at the moment. But you know what? Fuck it. Head off that way. Go get eaten. I think you would be doing us all a big favor." Jared turned, done with the group and the conversation.

He heard Tank grunt and had no time to brace for the impact as the football player tackled him from behind. Jared's body bent backward with such dexterity it looked as if Tank had snapped his spine. The two men collapsed to the floor, Tank threw a series of heavy, clumsy blows to the back of Jared's head.

Jared was able to cover up and fend off the worst of the attack and roll himself over in the process. Once he was on his back, his movements changed. He locked Tank's left arm—his dominant arm in their altercations so far—under his own and threw a heavy fist off the side of the man's head. Not aiming for the jaw, he made a solid connection with his temple and immediately saw the stunned look wash over Tank's face. Grabbing him by the shirt, Jared pulled Tank down to him while thrusting his head forward. The connection of thick bone with the soft cartilage of Tank's nose was a heavy one. The sound alone seemed to ring out, the crisp snap followed by the deep grunt as first shock and then pain radiated through the football player's head. Blood flowed in copious amounts, and Tank fell limp against Jared, who grunted and shoved the man off him.

Getting back to his feet, Jared waited for another attack. He was ready and willing to fight anybody who came near him, but they held back. Their eyes were focused over his shoulder, down the garden.

The young woman whose comments had started it all opened her mouth to scream, her trembling arm raised to point out the source of her fear. Before any sound could emerge, a thick stream of sour-smelling alcohol-infused vomit spewed from her mouth. She doubled over, emptying the contents of her stomach onto the ground.

Turning, Jared looked behind him. Down the garden, their arguments had disturbed the loved-up couple in the hot tub. Both had risen to face the group, making it clear why the girl had decided to abandon her stomach contents.

"Holy shit, look at that," the football jersey guy said, his words overflowing with fear and repulsion.

The pair had indeed been having a heavy session, only it was not just their lips that were locked. The naked girl stood, her curvy frame glistening wet in the shallow light. The mixture of water and blood made her look like a creature not of this world. Beside her, she held the boy she had fallen in love with, and whose face she had decided to eat. Even from a distance, and in the murky light, they could see she had torn through the man's face and shattered the bones, chewing right through to his brain. The grey-pink mass hung, half-devoured, from the gaping wound.

The zed woman made no effort to get out of the pool to attack them, but nobody wanted to wait long enough to find out why or challenge the thing to come and get them.

A crash from inside the house pulled their attention the other way. The barricade had given way, and a host of the undead, the majority of which were freshly woken partygoers—friends and fellow students, for the most part—spilled through the destroyed defenses, some stumbling only to be crushed by those who followed.

"Shit! What do we do?" Tank asked, his voice several pitches higher than normal.

"Run," Dwayne said, "around the side of the house."

They started to move, but before they made it halfway, the dead appeared there, too. Two shambling figures, nothing more than shadows in the dark, stopped the group in their tracks.

"Through the fields! The zeds are slow, so we just need to keep moving," Sam called, but it was too late. Panic was starting to set in.

One of the young women bolted from the group. She ran blindly toward the pack of zeds that had spewed from the house. At least fifteen had re-awoken from the carnage inside and followed their single remaining instinct toward the location of their next meal.

"Belle," Tank screamed, breaking into a powerful sprint.

"No, don't," Julie cried out, but Tank did not hear her.

The girl ran toward the group and would likely have avoided their initial charge had it not been for Tank's cries for her to stop. Turning around, she lost her footing and fell just as three hungry zeds stumbled down the steps from the house. They landed on her, their hands unceremoniously tearing into her flesh. The slender stomach was ripped apart, her navel piercing glinting as it was yanked out and up toward her face.

Blood bubbled in a flood from her gaping stomach, and like a pack of animals, the three zeds lowered their heads and lapped at the well they had struck. The girl continued to scream long after they shoveled her flesh into their mouths.

Tank let out a bellow as he saw Belle meet her fate. Shifting his direction slightly, he launched a flying tackle to the closest zed, hitting with such force they could hear the dead man's spine snap.

Tank landed hard and pushed himself back up to his feet, ready to take on the next creature. Five of them met him, their hands heavy and uncoordinated. While Tank put up a good fight, it ended swiftly when an undead hand forced its way into his mouth and ripped off his jaw. Tank remained standing long enough for his gaze to find the others. He cried out, but his deformed face was unable to construct any final words. He fell to the floor where hungry mouths were waiting.

"Fuck. This can't be happening," the second girl screamed, sinking to her feet, sobbing and rocking back and forth.

"We don't have time for this," Jared growled. "We need to move."

Sam crouched down by the girl, gently taking her by the shoulders and raising her head so that their eyes could meet. She then drew back her hand and slapped the girl across the face so hard that her head nearly spun from her shoulders.

The crying stopped, and the girl lay on the floor in silence, staring wide-eyed up at Sam and the others.

"We don't have time for you to be a princess, Princess," Sam growled.

Beside them, the jersey-wearing jock let out a laugh, a genuine sound of amusement.

"You find this fucking funny?" Jared snarled.

"Yo, sorry, dude. I'm with the program, really, but she called her princess, and well, her name is Leia," the man said, his laughter subsiding as he spoke.

"Okay, that's kinda funny, man," Dwayne said, nudging Jared with his elbow.

"I guess, but let's save the jokes. Get her on her feet, and let's book it," Jared said, looking over at the mounds of zeds that were feasting on the two carcasses. "Unless you want to end up like them."

Nobody said anything, but the group, which now numbered ten in total, moved away from the house. Once again, Sam and Dwayne took a dual-point, with Julie close behind them and Jared after her. While they were all working together, the segregation was still clear, for the second group hung back slightly, distancing themselves from Jared. Leah and the jersey-wearing jock walked hand in hand, with Ian beside them. Huddled close together after them were two more women and a slightly chubby man with a broken pair of glasses perched on his nose. One lens was cracked and the other missing completely.

Nobody spoke as they hurried off into the wilderness. There was a wet splash as the zed in the hot tub fell, but a quick look over their shoulders showed the woman sprawled in a heap on the floor.

"This way," Sam said, pointing to the left of the garden. "We can slip through here and around the fields."

"Where are we heading?" Dwayne asked her.

"I have no idea, but as long as we keep moving, we stand a chance," Sam answered. Looking up at him, she smiled, and as they walked, she slid her hand into his.

CHAPTER THREE

"We've got another cluster up ahead of us, sir," Sanjay Karumtha said as he adjusted the range on his binoculars.

"How many, soldier?" Lieutenant Lou Parker replied. In fifteen years of service, he had seen a great many things he wished he could forget. All of them paled in comparison to what he had witnessed in the past few weeks.

"I count three," Sanjay answered.

"I've got these ones, LT," Jerry Wilkes answered as the Hummer was brought to a stop.

Opening the doors, Jerry got out, followed by Maddie Staal. The only female in their unit, and the only female they knew to still be alive. Maddie was fiercer than the others combined. A fact they were all very well aware of. The fact that she was drop-dead gorgeous was therefore relegated to being useless information.

"You're never going to beat me," she whispered to Jerry as he drew his rifle up to his shoulder.

"Just you watch," Jerry said, shooting Maddie a wink as he turned his head and settled down to take the shot.

"Check the distance?" he asked.

"I've got nine hundred yards. The wind is low, almost nothing," Maddie replied. Nestled on the floor beside him, Maddie lowered her scope. "The floor is yours."

Jerry focused on the scene. He watched his targets. Their lumbering gait was impossible to predict, which meant tracking their movements in anticipation of a shot was that much more complicated.

The three post-humans, two men and a woman, were ambling through the barren fields of a farmhouse that looked long since deserted. Its owners having upped sticks and left long before the dead rose. Targeting them was easy, given the favorable conditions, and Jerry had no problem selecting his first kill. The shocking mop of bright pink hair made the woman an easy target, while the two men wore similarly branded shirts, advertising what Jerry assumed was a heavy metal band, or whatever. As far as he was concerned, it was all noise, indistinguishable from one another.

"Cutting it close, buddy," Maddie whispered. "No way you will make it."

Jerry ignored her goading and cleared his mind. He watched them a moment longer and pulled the trigger. The first shot from the Stealth Recon A1 blew out the pink lady's head, blowing it apart like a piece of rotting fruit. A shower of black blood and semi-liquefied brain matter flew from the exit wound, splattering against the two male zeds who did not even seem to notice. Pulling the trigger for the second time, Jerry watched as the first male zed's head disappeared in a puff of blood and bone and carried on through into the third. The damage tore the creature's face apart, shattering the skull. What little brain matter remained exited on the tail of the bullet, riding away in a cloud of blackened mist.

"Oh, no shit, you didn't just do that," Maddie gasped, unable to hide her excitement and enthusiasm.

"You know it. Two birds with one stone, yee-haw," Jerry cheered, slinging his rifle over his shoulder as he got back to his feet.

"Good shooting," Lou said, clapping the marine on the back as they returned to the vehicle. "What time did we get?"

"Eighteen seconds, from hitting the ground," Maddie said with a smile.

"Can I get a confirmation on that?" Lou asked, without looking at anybody in particular.

"I had the same, boss," Sanjay replied.

"I had seventeen," Benny Groffman, the fifth marine of their group spoke up.

"All right, I say we split the difference and seventeen-and-a-half seconds for Jerry. Where does that put him on the leaderboard?"

"He goes into second, behind Maddie, who still leads with seventeen seconds even," Benny answered, moving the dirty nametag up the side of the Hummer's interior.

"Unlucky, big boy. Looks like I get to keep your balls," Maddie said with a laugh.

The other marines joined in, enjoying the humor while the good mood lasted. They were soon on the road again. Meatloaf's *Bat out of Hell* was cranking out of the car's rudimentary stereo system, and all five marines were singing away to the tune.

The group had been stationed together for several years, and while Benny had never been under Lou's direct command, he was a well-known face around the base, and fit in easily with their crew. He had made the mistake of complimenting Maddie once, after having been assured by the lieutenant that she liked that sort of thing. He had worn his black eye with pride, especially after they told him what Maddie had done to the previous guy who tried to hit on her.

Ahead of them, the quiet road began to change. The littering of cars increased until they reached what could only be described as a blockade of sorts that blocked both lanes.

"What the hell?" Jerry said.

"Looks like they tried to protect themselves or something," Benny said.

"Waste of time. Surely they knew the dead were everywhere, not just marching down the road in some orchestrated assault," Maddie replied.

"They were scared," Sanjay said as the Hummer slowed. "They did what they needed to do in order to feel at peace." Out of the group, only Sanjay still held on to his firm beliefs in a god and reward for living a good life.

That was why he had not taken part in the shooting competition. He didn't want to make fun out of death. He said it was the Lord who sent the dead to teach them a lesson, and that once faith was restored, the world would return.

It had freaked the others out to hear him speak in such evangelical terms, but not even Maddie, a severely lapsed Catholic was willing to rip him for it.

"Can we go around it?" Lou asked.

"Not sure. We will need to get out and take a look," Benny said from behind the wheel. He opened the door and jumped out, leaving the engine running.

Lou followed from the passenger seat, drawing his M-1029. Known as the Major, the weapon had a six-inch blade with a serrated backbone. It was Lou's baby, and he kept it razor-sharp. It had already seen its fair share of blood, yet the steel still glinted, pristine; it was as if it were smiling at the idea of claiming some more.

They moved around either side of the road, the lieutenant with the Major, while Benny elected to use his survival ax, 'Bruiser'. The weapon had a three-and-a-quarter-inch wide black blade with a pick extending from the rear, meaning it could do damage on the forward and rearward strikes. The fifteen-inch length of the weapon also gave that little bit more room to maneuver, which had always been Benny's preferred position when it came to combat. Light on his feet, with reflexes quicker than anybody else in the unit, he worked best when he had a little room to play with.

They moved around the blockade, their steps slow and careful. Listening, they heard the undead moments before the three figures emerged. Two on Benny's side, and one obese man who came after Lou.

Benny struck out quickly, his ax cutting through the air with a melodious swoosh. The blade embedded itself in the skull of the woman, her lipless face held gnashing teeth that were chomping at the wind. It was only when he pulled the blade free that the full set of loose-fitting dentures fell from the old woman's mouth. They hit the concrete of the road and broke, several false molars flying in different directions.

Benny didn't wait, but adjusted his stance, jumped back a few steps, and repositioned himself to attack the second zed.

The tall, muscular creature before him must have been close to seven feet tall. His jet-black skin hid the hardened blood crust that had formed on his left arm. He moved forward awkwardly, the shredded skin of his left trap limited his range of motion of that side.

Using it to his advantage, Benny stepped to his right, ducked behind the creature and brought the pick end of the ax down on the back of the creature's head. The skull split with the fragile sound of a breaking eggshell. The tall zed dropped to its knees, black blood and a sour-smelling pus leaking around the wound the ax created. The weight of the dropping body pulled the blade free as the zed fell atop of the corpse of the old woman.

The others watched from inside the vehicle as the lieutenant engaged the dead man that half walked, half fell toward him. The obese man had a gut that hung down to his knees, and with the way his t-shirt had torn open, it gave the impression he had swollen considerably in death, exploding from within its confining polyester embrace. The tear in the material revealed four deep gouges that ran along his distended belly. The wounds continued to leak thick blackened blood, which had congealed to a consistency like that of cottage cheese.

Lou didn't waste any time. He grunted as he drove the knife in, thrusting it to the hilt right between the dead man's eyes. The force behind the strike was enough to bend the man over backward, causing his stomach to burst. The four tears ripped, opening up a watermelon-sized hole in the man's gut. The bubbling black mass of necrotic flesh flowered outward, spewing a deathly mix of blood, pus, and putrescence into the air. This was followed by semi-rotten chunks of intestines, still wet and soggy from the fluid they had been sitting in since the dead man rose.

Had it not been for the lieutenant's years of training and combat-honed reactions, he would have taken the rotten blast full to the face. As it was, he threw himself to one side, avoiding the majority of the spray.

"Oo-rah, way to go, LT." The others applauded from the Hummer, clapping as their lieutenant turned around, his legs tangled in a bloated string of sausage-like intestines. Walking back to the truck, he cleaned his blade on his pants and smiled at the others.

"That fat boy just couldn't control himself," Lou laughed, moving to get into the truck, but Benny closed the door.

Behind him, the others took greatly exaggerated breaths to add to the suspense.

"Very funny, dickwad. Now open the damned door." Lou pulled on the handle.

"No can do, boss. You're covered in zed guts. That means you got to ride freestyle until we can stop and get you hosed down," Benny said, pointing to the roof.

"Now, come on, Benny, it's barely a splash. Just a little bit of blood and rot. I wasn't bit or nothing." Lou tried to argue his case but started climbing before anybody could answer him.

The group inside the Hummer hammered on the roof with their fists as the lieutenant hauled himself into position.

"Punch it, Benny," Maddie called from the back seat, the entertainment in her voice bordering on childlike.

Benny pulled the car off the road, running over the downed zeds they had taken care of. Each one gave a soft squelch as the bodies burst from the pressure being applied to them. Pulling back onto the road, they drove through town, gathering the attention of enough of the local residents to bring them flocking toward the car.

"Guys, we need eyes left and right," Lou called from atop the vehicle.

Nobody heard the shot from his suppressed Glock 19, but they saw the closest zed to them jerk as a hole appeared where its left eye had once been. Thick, tar-like blood oozed from the hole before the dead man dropped to the floor, tripping up two others that had been close to him.

Opening the windows, Maddie and Jerry leaned out and started taking shots at any zed that came too close to the car. Benny continued to drive, his control of the car steady, and the speed fast enough to crush anything that got in their way.

One zed, who looked like a kid not long into their teens—if the pus-filled pimples that covered their face had indeed been there pre-death—appeared in front of the car, their arms raised, almost as if it were trying to hail them down like a cab.

Benny closed his eyes for a moment as the vehicle drove over the kid. Looking in the wing mirrors, Benny saw the body lying on the road, its belly flattened, but like a cartoon, its upper torso and legs were fine. Blood and gore leaked in all directions, and the creature continued to claw and snarl at the world around it.

"Jesus fucking Christ," Benny said.

"Hey, don't take the Lord's name in vain like that, dude," Sanjay said from behind the map.

"I just mean, that kid, he didn't die. I ran over him, a fucking kid, and he didn't die." Benny pushed away the guilt. He did what had to be done. He knew that and understood it, but everything had changed so suddenly, and kids were still kids in his eyes.

"They ain't kids no more, Benny," Jerry said as he turned to fire a shot at an approaching zed. The blast tore off the side of the dead man's head allowing thick clumps of grey-colored brain to cover the ground like rotten snow.

"Get us out of here," Lou called from above them. "I see more coming and don't want to take any chances. We are going to need this ammo later on."

"You got it, LT. Just hold on up there," Benny called as he shifted his driving style. His foot hit the gas and they rocketed down the street. They drove straight over anything that got in their way, and while splattered zed innards soon covered the windshield, Benny continued undeterred.

"Oh crap, look out," Lou called, slapping his hand down on the roof of the Hummer.

Benny saw it too and brought the vehicle to a swift halt. "Shit," he called out, looking around him for an alternative route.

"What is it?" Maddie asked as she reached out and stabbed a dead woman through the nose. "These things are getting too close for comfort, Benny."

"There's a blockage on the road. It runs all the way across," Benny said, opening his window to fire a trio of quick shots to take out the family of zeds who were closing in on him. A husband and wife, dressed in matching tracksuits, and an older child who looked a spitting image of his father, even down to the torn-out throat and slightly lolloping tongue.

"If you can double back, there is a side road we can take. It will be tight with this cumbersome vehicle, but we can follow that, make a hard left and hook around the back end," Sanjay said, dropping the map to his lap. He opened the door and shoved it as hard as he could, shattering the face of the zed licking his window.

"Got it," Benny said, throwing the Hummer into reverse.

As they sped backward, the lieutenant still holding onto the roof, firing as they went, the music changed and Meatloaf gave way to Kansas and a tune that felt almost prophetic as they mowed down the dead.

"There it is," Sanjay said, pointing out of his passenger window.

"Fuck, that's tight," Benny said as he turned the wheel, crushing the skull of a zed whose overturned wheelchair lay a few feet away.

"That's funny, I bet your daddy never had to say that," Maddie shot back as she slapped a fresh clip into her rifle and began to clear a path ahead of them.

Beside her, Jerry did the same, leaning out of the window to take out as many of the zeds between them and the small side street as he could.

"I hate the fucking suburbs," Benny growled mounting the curb to cut the corner, taking out a rose bed and a mailbox before tearing up two well-maintained lawns that had been recently fertilized with the blood of the damned.

They made it through the narrow street, which was little more than a widened alleyway that gave way to a set of small summer homes.

"Hard right," Sanjay called out just as Benny yanked the wheel and spun the beast of a car to the right. They clipped a parked car, obliterating the driver's side headlights.

"You reckon they want me to leave a note?" Benny asked, unable to help himself.

"Just keep driving. Your no-claims bonus is still safe," Jerry said from the back seat.

They made it through the winding streets of the suburb's inner sanctum and only once got stuck in a cul-de-sac that saw them make a very tight three-point turn amidst a fleet of brand new SUVs and minivans, all of which screamed lease rental.

The unit made it past the blockade and into a quiet, more expensive residential area. Gone were the small roads and warren-like pathways, and instead they were treated to large, sprawling lawns, and driveways filled with Mercedes and high-end Lexus cars. Three-story homes with adjoining garages, extensions, and no doubt swimming pools in the rear.

"We made it, boys," Lou called down to them, taking the chance to jump down to the ground. There were a few zeds lumbering around, but their numbers far less concentrated than on the other side of the barrier.

"That was closer than I wanted it to be," Jerry said, getting out of the vehicle.

"Aww, were you scared?" Maddie ribbed him.

"Guys." Benny tried to interrupt their games.

"Fuck you. I wasn't scared. Just saying it was closer than I wanted," Jerry shot back, defensive.

"Nice neighborhood. If we can make it through, then we have a clear run on into the city. Not sure we want to go that way, mind you," Sanjay said, joining the group outside the vehicle.

"Guys," Benny called louder this time.

"We need to recon. Check out the city and get an idea of how the virus' spread. That was the mission," Lou said, his voice unwavering.

"I know that, LT, but we've not heard anything from the base in three days. Besides, we can survey from outside the city. I mean, look at what we have seen so far. We know inside it's going to be worse. They can send a bird up to get a closer look," Sanjay suggested, not for the first time since they left the base.

"Guys!" Benny yelled, finally getting their attention. He too moved over to them, leaving the vehicle unoccupied. With all eyes turned toward him, Benny lowered his voice and spoke. "We've got a small problem."

"Small problems don't interest me, Benny," Lou answered.

"Okay, then we have a big fucking problem," Benny answered without hesitation.

"That's more like it." Lou smiled in spite of their situation. "Pray tell, what's gone up shit creek this time?"

Benny looked at the group and patted the Hummer. "This beast is thirsty. She ain't got much left. Maybe a couple of miles, at the most."

"Then we will trek out of glorious suburbia and find some gas. Or hell, we'll just take it from whatever we have parked here. There are enough options. I don't call that a big fucking problem." Lou waved his arms around in a sweeping gesture as if to draw their attention to the expensive cars.

"No, but there is more. The engine is fucked. I won't be sure what's up until I get under the hood, but it means we are going to be holed up here a while."

"All right, then we clear a house and claim it for our own. Clean up, chow down on whatever we can find, and regroup. Plenty of options all around us. I don't know what they call problems in your old unit, Benny, but you are with the Lucky Bastards now, and these, these ain't problems." Lou clapped their driver on the shoulder and gave a laugh. "Let's take one on each side of the street. Maddie, take Jerry here and sweep a couple of properties. Use your flashlight if he gets scared. Benny, Sanjay, come with me. We'll check 'em out, reclaim, and regroup."

The afternoon was drawing on, and the shadows of the houses loomed long over the ground. The dead milled around, but until then, had not shown much interest in the group. A few had wandered close by, but Maddie had taken care of them with swift efficiency. The first house was locked. They tried it once before taking a look through the letterbox. A set of snarling jaws greeted them, only not from the family dog, but rather from the family themselves. Three bodies stood in the hallway, snarling at the sound of the rattling door. A child, who could not have been long into the double digits appeared at the opening, her teeth snapping shut while her face crammed against the door as if trying to force her way through.

"Let's try around back. Maybe we can sneak in and take them out," Jerry said, looking at Maddie as she calmly closed the letterbox and stood staring up at the house.

"What I wouldn't give to live in a house like this," she said, as if the presence of the undead were now so commonplace they barely deserved a moment's thought.

"If we take care of these zeds, then maybe you can." Jerry winked at his partner, but there was something in her expression that held his smile at bay.

"Nah, man, I'm serious. I grew up with nothing. My dad was dead, killed in the Gulf, and my mom turned to drink to cope. I raised myself and my brother. It was toughen up or die. We're getting old now, and sometimes I think about the civilian life. Husband, kids, soccer practice, and a big-ass house like this." Maddie stopped talking as if catching her words and feeling embarrassed for them. "I don't know, I'm sorry. It's just these zeds, and the world now. It's changed, and well, maybe a normal life is gone."

They walked around the back of the house and pulled out their identical Honcho MT-122MR knives. Six-inch black steel blades, with a double stacked leather handle. Normally used as part of a survival kit, the weapons had already proven their worth in the field.

"Careful, I hear something," Jerry said as he opened the gate.

Maddie swept through first, and came to a sudden stop, with Jerry just beside her. The source of the noise was clear. The seething mass of flies and maggots rumbled even louder on the other side of the fence. The torn up remains of what had once been the family dog, lay rotting in the sun. The shriveled-up remnants of its insides trailing away from the carcass like snakes.

"Sorry, Rover," Jerry said under his breath as they moved around the side of the house. The garden swept back for quite some distance. Children's toys were scattered about the place, revealing something for all ages, a large sandbox and a climbing frame that would not have looked out of place in a community park. They also spotted a soccer goal that was not quite full-size, and a treehouse that had clearly been purchased rather than built.

"Fuck, I bet that damned tree house has more things in it than my old house on base did," Jerry joked.

A life-long bachelor, Jerry lived in the on-base accommodations, and for as long as Maddie had known him, never spoke about any love interests or family. He was very much a lone wolf.

That was part of the reason she was so attracted to him, but at the same time, his obvious inclination to be alone kept her from letting down her aggressive walls. Built as a means of self-preservation, she had spent enough of her youth stuck under the power of a succession of men, doing what she believed needed to be done in order to protect her brother.

"Check the windows. We need to know what we are walking into," Jerry whispered, pointing at the two wide windows that sat either side of the rear door.

The paved ground along the side of the house gave way to a raised patio area, complete with a garden furniture set and an oversized barbecue. They followed the bloody footprints that had been left by the family as they ambled back inside, splitting once they reached the threshold where Maddie took the near window, and Jerry the far. It was hard to make much of anything and took them a moment to realize some sort of screen was lowered on the inside, blocking any clear view.

"Looks like we are going in blind," Maddie said, looking over at Jerry.

"Ain't that always the way?" Jerry replied, as he tried the door. Neither was surprised to find it open.

"Be on guard, there is bound to be more than just three of them in there." The warning was not necessary. Jerry knew that Maddie knew the dangers, but he felt the need to offer his protection, not because she couldn't handle herself, but because he couldn't bear the thought of anything happening to her. He had seen enough fucked up shit in his years to appreciate it when something good came into his life.

Having seen his father kill his mother in a drunken fit, only to have him slit his throat before his seven-year-old son's eyes, Jerry had grown up quick and grown up hard. He closed himself off from those around him. Turned away by the little family he had left, he bounced around the system for a while before eventually running away. The streets honed him; they taught him aggression, but also respect. A few severe beatings, gained for looking at the wrong person in the wrong way, soon made him understand the system and the rank that came with age and status.

Had it not been for a chance encounter with an off-duty marine, who broke up a fight Jerry had been in, the streets would have undoubtedly killed him long before now. Enlistment had saved his life in more ways than he dared think.

"Got it. Sweep this room, I'll take left, you right," Maddie said, adrenaline beginning to surge.

Jerry didn't answer, there was no need. They moved off, disappearing into the house. The kitchen was vast and spacious. A marble-topped center island replaced the more standard dining room table, and countertops lined the three sections of wall to the immediate left. The look was completed by quite possibly every piece of kitchen apparatus known to man.

To the right, a solid wood cabinet stood against the wall, flanked by two smaller units, which together, covered the entire wall. The tall ceiling housed two ventilation fans with two lights apiece. The tiles on the floor were tainted red with blood, and a pool had congealed between the sink and the central island. The outline of where it had spread before shrinking away stained the tiles like beetroot.

Maddie didn't say a word as she moved to the left, skirting around the island, checking to make sure the coast was clear. She raised her hands and signaled a green light, and Jerry set off into the hallway.

The long hall extended down toward the main front hall where the three snarling zeds still stood, focused on the door. Jerry knew it wouldn't last. As soon as they caught wind of fresh meat, they would turn and descend like a pack.

A dining room sprouted from the right-hand side of the hall. The open room housed nothing more than a sideboard cupboard and a dining table with enough seating for at least a dozen people. It was easy to see the room was unoccupied, but in the interest of being thorough, Jerry slipped inside. The soft carpet of the room felt strange beneath his boot. Even before the world went to shit, Jerry could not recall the last time he had stood on anything other than tile or linoleum when inside.

There were two tall windows in the room, the very ones he had peered through from the outside just moments before. A large clock was slowly ticking on the wall to his left. The table, which was not set, had place settings before each stool, and only served to emphasize the emptiness of the house. The dead did not count; they were gone the moment their hearts stopped beating, just as it always had been. Only now, they rose back up and ate you, but it didn't change the facts. Dead was dead. Gone was gone.

Jerry heard something in the doorway and spun around. Maddie looked at him and nodded. He returned the gesture, and together they continued on their sweep of the house. There were two other rooms, one on each side. A spacious sitting room and a study. Neither could be accessed without alerting the three dead family members who had lost interest in the door and so returned to their near-catatonic shamble.

Stuck in such close quarters, they barely moved at all, their motion reduced from a shuffle to something that closely resembled a sway, a gentle slow dance performed without a partner. They moved no more than a few inches in either direction before swaying back the other way again.

For a moment, both Maddie and Jerry stood staring at them, their knives at the ready but lowered. Both saw it, and a quick meeting of their gaze confirmed the other felt the same. The sadness and loneliness of the house were the driving factors, far outweighing the fear, that, while subdued, still lurked just beneath the surface of it all.

The moment did not last long. Their scent inevitably reached the nostrils of the youngest zed, whose sudden animation seemed almost fast by comparison and only served to alert the other two. Their snarls grew, and like ferocious watchdogs, they turned and set after the intruders.

The child moved without issue, its injuries restricted to a single bite mark on the arm. Nothing a long sleeve shirt would not have hidden. Maddie finished him off with a swift and merciful blow that came from above, splitting his crown and piercing what remained of his brain.

The parents showed more extensive injuries, the mother hobbling on one foot, the right leg ending in a weeping stump of mangled meat, while the father, or at least the male of the pair, was missing his throat and upper trap area, which caused his head to hang with an inquisitive tilt.

Neither Jerry nor Maddie were in any rush, and so waited for the dead to reach them, the ulterior motive being to try to draw out anything else that may have been waiting in the adjoining rooms.

No further undead folks joined in the fun, and so it was left to a two-on-two showdown. The fight was so uneven, it was almost unfair. Maddie and Jerry finished their respective zeds off in near synchronicity, both plunging their Honcho blades through the temple up to the hilt.

"Well, that was easy," Jerry said before a strange wailing sound came down to them from the upstairs.

Both of them froze. "That's not what I think it is," Jerry said.

"I ... we have to go check, don't we?" Maddie asked. The look in her eyes was pleading with Jerry, begging him not to answer the question.

"We could just leave it behind," Jerry said, offering Maddie the out she was looking for.

For a while, neither spoke. All they heard was the growling wail coming through the baby monitor planted on the small cabinet by the front door.

"We can't, not ... not if it is what ... well, you know," Maddie stammered.

"I can go check if you want." Jerry was not sure which unsettled him more. The sound from the floor above them, or the look on Maddie's face. He had never seen her rattled or even so much as a little bent out of shape.

"No, we'll check it out, no telling what else could be up there," Maddie said, catching herself.

She closed her eyes for a few moments, and when they opened again, the Maddie he knew, was back. The cold eyes of a killer and the stony face of a woman who was in control.

They moved up the stairs slowly, ready for anything. With each step they rose, the wailing sound seemed to grow on an exponential curve.

The upper floor of the house was one long corridor with five rooms sprouting from it, and a flight of stairs leading up to another floor. The plush carpet under their feet crunched intermittently as their footfalls fell on the blood-encrusted sections.

"What the hell happened here?" Maddie whispered as they stared at the blood-smeared walls. Gory handprints marked out the passage of someone and led them beyond the empty bedrooms and bathroom, and right up to the door that housed the source of their nightmarish screams.

They stood against the door, neither wanting to open it for fear of what they would find. Jerry raised his hands, giving a thumbs up to his partner. Maddie saw the gesture and gave a slight nod in response. Jerry reached for the door handle and gave a gentle push.

The door swung inwards, the special hinge coverings giving the door a bit more resistance, no doubt to keep small fingers safe and sound.

The room was smaller than the others, but not by much, and decorated almost entirely in pink, from the pale walls to the darker shaded stencils that adorned the wall opposite them. To the immediate left was a short wall with a wash basin and mirror. Beside it was a baby changing table, adorned with all manner of products, from lotions and talcum powder to special baby shampoos and wash gels. A plush cuddly toy, itself the size of a small child, sat guard over the bounty.

The door was on the right-hand side of the room, meaning the majority of the open space extended to the left. A wardrobe adorned with stickers of unicorns and faeries sat along the door-side wall, and the plush carpet once again told of the affluence of the family who had lived there. The crib was an expensive, solid construction, painted white with a pink netting that hung suspended from the ceiling.

"She was their princess," Maddie whispered, unable to take her eyes away from the crib.

Jerry looked at her and did a double take as he saw the tears reflected in them. Thick, blackness-inducing curtains hung before both windows on the long rear wall and the far side one. Those by the far window were drawn shut, but the others were pulled back and held in place by restraints a darker shade of pink than the curtains themselves.

At the sound of their approach, the howls of the baby in the crib increased, reaching what could only be described as a fever pitch.

"You ready?" Jerry asked as they approached the crib. They could see the occupant moving around through the material.

"No," Maddie answered, but reached forward toward the net drape.

Pulling it back, the stench that wafted up to them was overpowering. A heady concoction of vomit, excrement and the almost standard scent of rot, which hung in the air, not only inside the house but outside of it too. The world was lost to the concept of fresh air, as no matter where you were, the breeze carried with it the taint of death. A continuing reminder that nobody was safe, and most likely never would be again.

Leaning over the crib, Maddie took one look and withdrew, her tough shell finally cracking. It broke Jerry's heart to see it happen, and under such conditions, but he could not help but feel a little relieved, for it showed that Maddie was not just the tough lone wolf she painted herself to be.

Jerry took a breath and leaned over the crib. Unsure what to expect, and taking Maddie's extreme reaction, he expected the worst, but what he saw went so far beyond that, it made his imagination look like the colorful drawing of a child.

The child lay on its back, its bald head as white as the sheets she lay on had been. Dark veins snaked over its face, marking it like a road atlas, the black blood that filled them had thickened, causing them to rise up and bulge beneath the infant's fragile skin. Its face had sunken, the eyes burrowed deep into its skull. It looked as if the baby had two black eyes. Its body was equally frail, the exposed arms and legs that protruded from the filth-encrusted onesie were similarly tattooed with veins.

The creature—for Jerry reminded himself that it had ceased to be a baby the moment its tiny heart stopped beating—was thrashing around on the mattress, covered in a thick half-solidified layer of its own waste. Blood smeared its face from where it had eaten. The stumps at the end of its legs were black with rot. The feet were missing, chewed away by the few teeth the baby had in its mouth. What remained of a big toe lay beside the creature's head, the aroma of the decayed flesh wafting and teasing the baby who could not reach the tasty morsel.

Jerry felt his stomach tighten, the acidic burn and excess salivation that preceded vomit, hit him like a blow to the head. He watched, horror-stricken, as the infant chewed through its own hand. Two fingers were removed sending blackened tar-like blood spurting from the wounds. Delighted, the greedy infant sucked it down without hesitation.

Jerry turned away from the bed, sending a long, arcing stream of brackish vomit across the room. It projected so far that it streaked the wall as well as staining the carpet. Maddie stood back, staring at the crib, unmoving. Her eyes just as vacant as the creatures they were fighting against.

The sight of the baby had broken the walls and allowed the full realization of the world to hit home.

She started to shake as she stared at the bed. In her mind, she could not replace the image of the self-mutilated baby, so tiny and delicate, yet still consumed by such uncontrollable bloodlust. On top of that, her mind chose that moment to throw her a flashback to the time in Afghanistan when a peasant woman had left her baby at a checkpoint. The child had been screaming in its baby carriage. Her best friend on the base, Maria Gonzalez had responded to the cries and picked the baby up. The pressure switch for the bomb the baby lay upon blew Maria into so many pieces they didn't have anything tangible to ship home.

It was the one moment from her career that continued to haunt Maddie, and as she listened to the zed baby's shrieks, drifting away into an abyss of terrifying numbness, she knew that the nightmare now had a friend.

"Jerry," Maddie spoke, her voice sounded distant, not her own. "Jerry, come on, let's leave it. There are plenty of other houses."

She moved forward, her legs not her own. Everything was falling apart, and suddenly the idea of being outside, surrounded by the dead or not, was the most appealing thing in the world.

She reached out and lay a hand on Jerry's shoulder. She could feel his body shaking, and it grounded her. Her own fears were okay; she was allowed to be scared, or to feel the weight of the horrors they had seen.

"Can you walk away from that?" he asked, looking Maddie in the eye.

Maddie hesitated, steeling herself; reminding herself that the people the dead once were, were gone.

"Yes," she said, unaware of the emotion that choked her words.

"I don't believe that any more than you do," Jerry said.

Standing up slowly, he turned and looked back at the crib. The dead baby had silenced itself, for the time being.

"It can't hurt anybody in there. What if we seal up the house?" Maddie suggested.

"Someone will get in, and if it bites even one person, that would be on us," Jerry answered, his voice resigned to the act he was going to commit.

He took half a step toward the crib, his hands frozen by his blade, but unable to close around the handle.

"You don't have to watch," he said to Maddie.

"Why, because I'm a woman?" she said, her voice coming from beside him.

He didn't rise to the bait. He understood she was saying it to distract herself. Creating a wall that would keep the act and the lingering memories of it at bay for as long as possible.

"Then we do it together," he said, finding the strength in her presence to draw his blade. Even the metal seemed dull, as if not truly up for the task.

The undead baby lay in its crib, sleeping, of all things. Its thumb in its mouth, not in hunger, but in what passed for slumber.

"Oh man, it looks vaguely peaceful," Maddie said, catching her tears before they could fall. "It's not too late."

Jerry raised his knife and moved over the crib, lowering the weapon on the other side of the bars.

The baby opened its eyes: the black, dead, shark-like eyes, and immediately began to groan and claw at the air. Its small hands found the knife, clutching at the sharp blade, which sliced through the chubby fingers without effort.

"Fuck," Jerry said, as the baby drew the blade into its mouth, budding milk teeth clamping down on the metal with tiny clicks.

He watched and could not help but wonder if it was deliberate.

"It wants to die, it wants to be put at peace," he said, choking on the words. Tears flowed freely, and he didn't care.

"It can't think. But it deserves peace," Maddie said, as she reached over and placed her hand over Jerry's.

Both turned their head, so they did not have to watch the final moments of the infant's life, but the silence that followed its end was the most powerful thing either had experienced.

They left the house through the front door. They stared at the floor, ambling mindlessly like the dead they were trying to stave off.

The rest of the group appeared across from them. Benny was covered in blood, his ax still clenched in his fist, lumps of rotting flesh still clinging to the blade.

"We've cleaned out two houses across the way. One was infested, but Benny here got 'em all. Son of a bitch is like a fucking animal when he gets going." The lieutenant clapped the blood-soaked driver on the shoulder and gave a laugh.

It was only then he noticed the looks that Jerry and Maddie wore. It was a look he had seen before. The look that soldiers get when they are broken.

"What happened in there?" he asked.

Neither spoke. They stood with the rest of their small unit, grey-faced and silent. To observers, they would have looked more like the dead than the living and would most likely have been left behind.

"Jerry, Maddie, talk to me. What happened in there?" Lou asked, his voice soft, no longer that of the tough military man, but now the mentor, and confidant.

Jerry raised his head first, his tear-stained eyes looking at each man in turn, holding their gaze long enough for his pain to be understood.

Opening his mouth, he took a long, deep breath, and told them everything that had happened.

By the time he was finished, the entire group looked as if they had been told their mothers had died. All jokes and joviality were gone, stripped away by the cold facts of the new world.

"You did the right thing. This world isn't the place for their kind, and a ... a ... young'un doesn't deserve that fate. Come on, let's get off the street. We've got two clean over there, and enough food to give us all a good meal," Lou said, placing a hand on both Jerry and Maddie's shoulders. "We'll fill our bellies and rest up. We can move on in the morning."

They followed him, falling in line with the rest of the group. Together, they disappeared into one of the buildings the group had cleared. The odor of death hung in the air, but they didn't care. Stepping over the corpse of an obese man, whose stomach seemed to be melting in all directions over his frame, they moved into the kitchen.

Sanjay and Benny got to whipping up a meal. Mostly tinned goods, but after the food they had grown used to eating while out on deployment in God knew where, it all tasted like heaven.

They ate in the living room and spoke as if they were watching TV. Shouting random answers to questions they recalled from the various TV quiz shows they watched before things changed.

Slowly, the gravity of the day melted away, as it had to do if they were to carry on. Even Maddie and Jerry seem brighter, although neither truly spoke.

As night fell, none of the soldiers were willing to pass up the chance to enjoy the comforts of a real bed. Spreading across the two houses, there were enough places for them all to sleep comfortably without having to worry about being climbed over and prodded in the back by a rifle butt or stray knee that was sent flying by some dreaming soldier.

Jerry tossed and turned, but despite the soft mattress and the floral bedspread, both of which made it feel as if he were trapped inside a cloud, he could not settle. His mind continued to show him the images he had tried so hard to force away.

He heard the others snoring, an impressive din that seemed to resonate through the otherwise empty house.

The new world ushered in a new, lifeless atmosphere. Even though the house was decorated, furnished, and filled with marines, it felt empty and hollow.

Turning once more, Jerry sprang bolt upright in his bed, his eyes wide and his revolver in his hand. He stared at the figure in his room.

Maddie did not flinch. She stood in the doorway, staring at Jerry, her own eyes just as wide, and intense as his. Their stares locked for a moment before Jerry lowered the gun.

Maddie walked into the room and closed the door. She was as naked as the day she was born. Her slender, toned body seemed to glow in the moonlight streaming through the open curtains. She didn't say a word as she walked up to the bed. Likewise, Jerry remained silent as he threw back the covers and welcomed her to him.

Their lovemaking was silent, and it was hard, almost brutal. The end of the world as they knew it had damaged the foundations they had so heavily relied upon. Everything they had locked away for decades was now starting to seep through the cracks.

There was no passion or tenderness to their congress, and when it was over, Maddie slipped from the bed and walked back to her own room without ever muttering so much as a word. Likewise, Jerry merely rolled over with his back to the door and fell asleep within moments.

CHAPTER FOUR

When the alarm went at four the next morning, Taron wanted nothing more than to roll over and go back to sleep. He couldn't, and he knew that, but he wanted to, nonetheless.

Getting up at the butt-crack of dawn was not something strange to him. A surgeon by trade, he had worked his fair share of crazy hours and double shifts, especially during his residency and during general training. Whenever the alarm sounded in his life, Taron wanted to go to roll over, but he was instantly awake, alert and ready for anything. Be it a multi-car pile-up with blood and limbs littered across the highway, a heart-attack at a hot dog eating contest, or simply to head out and watch, to make sure the undead didn't come chomping at their door. He had seen and done it all in his years.

Rolling out of his bed, he dropped to the floor in the middle of the bunker and blasted out a quick set of fifty press-ups, fifty crunches, and fifty squats, stretched his back and headed out the door. There was no time for coffee, no time for a quick bite to eat. Hector had been on duty for the past three hours and needed to be relieved from the watch.

They had tried several combinations for guard duty, before settling on three-hour watches. It was hard, especially that last half an hour, but it worked way better than their initial four hours, and the hourly switch was not long enough for people to rest when off duty.

Three-hour shifts meant they each had two guard rotations per day, which worked out well with the other duties.

Taron didn't mind the guard shift, the quiet time actually relaxed him. Only twice had he been forced to fire his weapon, and on each occasion, the single zed had been the only post-human he had seen.

After the herd movement from the day before, he was sure there would be a few more sightings today, but they had made the agreement, much to Hector's disappointment, they would only shoot if necessary. Zeds could pass them by unharmed if they remained oblivious, or whatever word described a postie's ability to move by them without noticing their presence.

Taron understood why Hector disagreed with their stance. Any zed stood a chance to infect, tens of people, possibly more, before it got taken out. To let them live was effectively signing a death warrant for someone else.

Yes, to shoot and miss, possibly drawing the attention of a group or even a herd of them, that would spell the end of them all. Their camp was well stocked, but at the end of the day, they were just four people and one kid. They would not stand much hope against a large force of the undead.

Leaving the shelter, he looked around, his hand already curled around the blade of his knife. He knew Hector was watching, but it always paid to be cautious. All it took was one moment for something to slip through unseen.

While none of them had really held any long conversations on the subject, Taron knew the dead were not the only threat lurking in the world. For now, they were the priority, but there would come a time that survivors fought back, that people grouped together and fought for what they needed. It was human nature, and with the laws of modern society purged from existence by the sweeping hordes of the resurrected dead, there was nothing enforcing control on anybody.

Welcome to the wastelands, he thought to himself, remembering a catchphrase from some wrestling tag-team.

As he crossed over to the lookout post, confident that the coast was clear, Taron let his mind wander back to the time before, which although fairly recent in terms of linear time, felt as if it had occurred several lifetimes ago. Wrestling had been something Taron watched with his father and had grown up enjoying. As he became an adult, then a doctor, and then a surgeon, he never lost his love for it. If anything, he believed he appreciated it and enjoyed it more as an adult. Understanding the process, knowing the secrets only increased his admiration for what the men would do to their bodies.

He even had tickets to *WrestleMania* one time, a couple of years back. He bought them as a surprise for his father. Front row seats, ringside.

His father was sick, dying in fact. There was nothing anybody could do to save him. Taron knew this. He knew it from talking to the doctors treating his father. He knew it from his own knowledge, having read the medical charts and files during one of their many hospital visits together. Worst of all, he knew it as a son. The sense of living on borrowed time was a sobering one.

As he knocked on the door to the lookout post, he took a deep shuddering breath. For the feeling he had as a son for his father were the same feelings he had now. Borrowed time … it was all any of them had.

Hector opened the door, his rifle in his hand. His sharp-featured face and cold, steel-grey eyes were stained pink with fatigue, but he never allowed it to truly show.

"Anything to report?" Taron asked as he stepped inside, allowing Hector to close and lock the door.

"Nothing really. Had a damned fox trying to get into the back building, but I chased it away," he said, dropping into one of two chairs in the lookout. He had a flask of coffee with him, which Taron eyed silently.

"No zeds?" Taron asked.

"Nope, quiet as a snowy morning." Hector smiled. He seemed relaxed, in spite of what had happened to them only hours before.

"Good, now go inside and get some rest, man. We've got a busy day ahead of us, after the havoc of yesterday," Taron said, as good as hustling Hector out of the door.

Once he was alone, Taron settled down into the lower level and got comfortable.

The lookout post they had created was an iron building with deep-seated foundations beneath a framework of interwoven tree branches, essentially a wicker construction, atop which they layered dirt and mud, then grass, building it up over time to look like a hill. An out of place hill, which, given the nature of their current enemy, did not draw any unwarranted attention.

Simple in design, it had four lookout spots, one on each side, with small slats built into the structure to allow the on-duty guard a good line of sight at all angles. While the structure sat close to ground level, they had actually raised the floor about a foot off the ground. The intention was to create four sections of ground-level space where the guards could lay down and watch for any threat. The central raised island connected to the door, the only entry or exit point in the structure, held two chairs and a small table. There was no need for anything else. For the night shift, they had night-vision scopes on two of the rifles, and there was an old-school oil lamp for use in case of emergencies.

As he got comfortable, the pitch of night begging to lift, Taron felt himself relax. Not to the point of dereliction of duty, but simply because when on watch, life became even simpler. You watched, you waited, and you shot when needed.

The time drew on, and not long after five, he saw Henry appear outside, taking his now customary morning job around the compound. The site was not large but running on the inside of the perimeter for half an hour was certainly enough to start the day right and keep people in condition for life in the new world.

Taron watched Henry run for a moment but returned his eyes to the tree line. While they had four stations, the main focus was always the campsite's main entryway. It was the weakest part of their current fortification, and often a topic of conversation. In the long run, they knew they would need to reinforce the entire site, that or pack up their belongings and move completely. An option none of them every truly entertained, but always kept in reserve for when the conversation inevitably came around.

As he sat, and the new day dawned around him, Taron even allowed himself to feel content with things.

He had lost loved ones and friends. Even the deaths of those few people in his life through circumstance, and whose involvement he cared little for, were felt as losses. They had all been through it, but now, with life being rebuilt on the other side, he realized that much like grief at the loss of a loved one, the stages for the loss of one way of life were no different.

His grief was over, denial and anger long in the past, forced there by the unwavering and unsympathetic onslaught of the damned. Now, having accepted their fate, he found comfort in the simple things life had to offer. He had a place, a community that he belonged to and while it lasted, they were determined to make the most of it.

All he wished for was a radio and some tunes. What he wouldn't give to hear some music, just to break up the silence of being on watch.

After an uneventful three hours, Taron was relieved by Vanessa, who, while not one to venture outside of the camp without severe cause to do so, had proven herself to be a dead shot with both the rifle and a bow and arrow. Yet oddly enough, she found the crossbow uncomfortable and her aim suffered as a result.

"How are things?" she asked, the standard greeting at the changing of the guard.

"Quiet as can be. Didn't even get a sniff of movement through the trees. Hector mentioned a fox or something sniffing around the rear building, but I didn't see anything. Whatever it was, it's long gone now." Taron gave Vanessa the run down on things, before leaving her to her duties.

He was ravenous with hunger and could already taste the coffee before he opened the door to the shelter.

The smell hit him as soon as he walked in. Spam fritters and fresh bread, char-toasted to perfection.

They had run out of butter a week or two earlier but had hopes that they would be able to create some form of substitute from the milk provided by their goat.

The goat and three chickens were kept in a small building behind the shelter. The zeds seemed relatively uninterested in the animals, and so the group had been building a small pen that allowed the animals some freedom.

Vanessa was the homesteader of the group. A good cook, and having grown up in a rural farming environment, she knew her way around animals, from raising them to slaughtering them.

"Just in time," James said as he looked up from his plate of food. "I was going to start without you."

The kid smiled and his continued enthusiasm for each day highlighted exactly what it meant to be a child.

Even though he was fully aware of everything that had happened, he still looked forward to tomorrow as if he were just at home watching cartoons on the sofa.

"I'd never miss a meal. Especially not with him around, he'd steal my last piece of bread, and make me think I gave it to him," Taron whispered and pointed as Hector emerged from his bunk.

He looked far from rested after his three-hour nap. None of them did. The weight of life hung heavy on their shoulders. Nobody slept peacefully through the night anymore. Even James had, on occasion, woken up screaming, his dreams plagued by nightmares.

The three and a half men sat and ate in relative silence. The bread was still the good side of stale and eating it meant that a new loaf was needed. In turn, the prospect of freshly baked bread improved the quality of the current piece they were eating.

Besides, it was not the food the adults looked forward to. Sure, sustenance was important, and none of them would have voluntarily skipped a meal, no matter what the ingredients were, but coffee ... coffee was where their minds went to.

Rationing had been put into effect from the very start. They knew they needed to do everything to conserve their resources.

"Why give ourselves the chance to be wasteful early on, when we need to think long term?" It had been Vanessa who spoke sense into them and instituted the rations. They played it smart, using the first week to be rather liberal, and slowly tightened it with each passing day.

Being rationed down to a single cup of coffee every meal was tough, even for Taron, who had never been a coffee drinker in all of his days on Earth, preferring tea or cola, even during the crazy double-double shifts he had pulled when first starting out his residency. Yet now, with the end of the world behind them, and the daunting task of rebuilding up ahead, coffee had suddenly become his lifeblood.

He savored the way the rich, black fluid smelled, especially when coming in from the cold. The bitter taste, which burned slightly as it went down. They had run out of milk even before they did butter, and while the goat provided a little, it was agreed that it should be used for cooking purposes, rather than tarnishing the beautiful darkness that was their favorite beverage.

"Life in a cup," Hector said as he placed his coffee back on the table. The steam rising from the cup said it was still scalding hot, yet he had effortlessly downed half the contents without so much as a flinch.

Even James nursed his own smaller cup, diluted with extra water, to take away the brew's aggressive edge.

Once everybody had eaten, James cleared the table, and they all sat down to plan the day. Routine was key for them all and starting with breakfast and a meeting had proven to be the most effective manner with which to work.

"We need to have a look at the fence and see how much damage was done yesterday," Henry started, recalling the post-human with the barbed wire wrapped around his legs. "I also think it is time we started thinking about additional reinforcements. There has to be some way we can fortify things without making it look like we are building a fortress. We don't want to draw any unnecessary attention."

"We need to use the trees. Cut 'em down, spike the ground, maybe dig some bear pits too," Hector said as he rolled a cigarette. The only real smoker in the group, Hector loved rolling his own cigarettes, and already had plans to start growing his own tobacco as soon as things settled to the point where they became a real, self-sustaining community.

"I know we had some discussions way back when, but with the rules changed now, I don't see why not. Bear pits, I'm a bit apprehensive about, but reinforcing the main entry points around the perimeter make sense to me. Let's first check out the damage. Repair it as best we can and then take it from there," Henry answered, looking around the table at each of them in turn.

"Daddy, can I go with you?" James asked.

"No," Henry answered quickly. "Your mother would kill me; besides, it is too dangerous out there for you. You need to stay here, help your mother. Plus, I have some jobs for you, jobs that only you can do."

The disappointment on the kid's face was clear, and he made no attempt to conceal it.

"You can't keep him wrapped up forever," Hector said, speaking up as he ran the paper along the tip of his tongue and effortlessly rolled the tube through his fingers; his eyes not on the job at hand, but rather watching the others around the table.

"We're not having that discussion again." Henry's voice was firm.

"But, Dad," James began, only to hold his tongue upon catching a stern look from his father.

"Kid's gotta learn sometime," Hector said.

"Not today," Henry replied.

"Better today than tomorrow, you never know what's going to happen," Hector reiterated.

"I said no," Henry slammed his palm down on the table and ended the conversation. "James, I need you to check out the rear building. Hector said there was a fox sneaking around. I need you to inspect it and fortify it where you can. We have some chicken wire in storage. Use it sparingly, but against any places you think are weak."

"Yes, sir." James couldn't help but sound disappointed, even if the task he had been given was far more important than his usual duties.

"Hector, you and I will head out to take a look at the damage on the perimeter. Taron, I want you to tend the animals, and check on the goat. That wound on her leg still hasn't healed and I don't want to risk losing her." Henry gave the orders, and the group reacted like the well-oiled machine they were. "I'll be back for my stint on watch. After we eat lunch, I want you, Taron, to take Hector and walk the perimeter to the rear. Check for any signs of yesterday's herd and see if you can't find some of those fruit bushes again. I don't know how you do it, but you always manage to find them."

With their duties arranged, they drained the last of their allotted coffee rations and headed out.

As with every day, there was a lot to do, and never any time to waste.

CHAPTER FIVE

"Ronnie, watch out!" Jared called out, finally referring to the jersey-wearing jock by his first name.

Ronnie spun to face the shambling dead man approaching him, raised his makeshift weapon, and froze. The man had not died a good first death. From the tattered look of his face, a motorbike wreck would have been the first thing to come to mind. The shredded skin and gravel embedded remains were a solid indicator, while the wrecked bike that lay just behind him, still holding on to the arm that had been severed at the moment of impact, merely served to emphasize the point.

"Kill it," Leah called, her voice seeming to spur Ronnie back to life.

Raising the crowbar, he brought it crashing down on the top of the zed's skull, splitting it in two, sending a thick black goo cascading from the gash. As he tugged the weapon free, sticky globs of decayed brain matter clung to the metal. As he pulled it back over his shoulder, a few clots of blood splattered against Abby's leg.

Abby screamed while her friend Kate and their painfully obvious gay best friend Jack both tried to hush her.

"Be quiet, girl, plcase." Jack held his hand over Abby's mouth. "We don't want more of them coming this way."

Abby calmed herself and nodded, and while Jack's meaty hands hid half of her face, the terror in her eyes was enough to show them she understood the danger.

"We need to keep moving. We're on the edge of the city, and well, those things are everywhere. If they find us …" Samantha faced the group and did her best to hurry them along.

While there had been no vote, or even time for a discussion on the subject, the group had somehow fallen behind Samantha and Dwayne's lead. Julie and Jared came close behind them. The others who had been rescued from the frat house followed; apart from Ronnie, they were lost sheep; mourning the death of their friends, and still traumatized by the forced acceptance of what had happened.

Not long after they left the house, they added another group to theirs. A family of three brothers, who were also trying to leave the city.

The youngest of the three was injured and collapsed as they walked. The others insisted on carrying him between them.

Nobody saw him come back until it was too late. He chewed off his brother's ear in a frenzied attack before dragging him to the floor and sinking his teeth into his throat. Blood spurted in all directions, like a drilled-through water main. Fountains of dark crimson had jumped higher than could be believed, and for a moment everybody froze, shocked by what they had witnessed.

That was all the time it took for the second brother to die. Reaching, he pulled his two siblings apart, and in a rush of feral aggression, the younger brother turned on the eldest, and with no effort at all, ripped away the lower jaw and buried his face in the bloody mess left behind.

Nobody had spoken about the three since. Too much had happened in the hours since leaving the safety of their party house. None of the group could cope with or process the depth of loss surrounding them. It still ate away at them, nibbling through the dark parts of their subconscious, but for the immediate future, it was buried far enough away from the surface not to matter.

They crept through the edges of the city, avoiding the high-density areas. Yet still, the dead surrounded them. Groups, hundreds strong in places, reacted to their passing, but were so slow, the group had disappeared before any of the zeds made it close enough to them.

The streets were a mess, abandoned cars dotted the roads while the burned out remains of several multi-vehicle pile ups blocked the larger intersections they passed.

Several of the wrecks had passengers still inside. Snapping and snarling at the grime and gore-covered windows. One particular wreck involved a truck, three minivans, and, judging by the body parts and drying pool of blood, more than a few pedestrians.

The windscreen of the truck was shattered. The burly man who had been behind the wheel had burst through the glass, his skin ripped open by the hungry glass teeth. His body reared upwards pulling his blackened, bloated face from the front of the vehicle. He had a long beard, stained red, and a shard of glass embedded in his throat poked through the matted hair. His eyes were grey and as he caught the scent of the group, he began to thrash.

His movements shook his entire body, causing it to slip farther and farther through the hole in the window. His skin dragged over the razor-sharp shards, tearing with an audible rip. Black blood dripped down onto the bodies beneath him, seeming to wake them as a result. One woman, whose oversized breasts flopped down either side of her considerable stomach—they were large and saggy enough to touch the ground on either side of her—began to thrash in an attempt to collect the dripping rotten goodness in her mouth.

"Would you look at that," Ronnie said with a laugh, pointing at the woman. "She's gagging for it."

"Eww, that's gross." Leah slapped Ronnie on the arm and turned away.

"Come on, babe, I'm just joking." Ronnie hurried after Leah, grabbing her and pulling her into his arms.

"We can't joke about this, dude," Ian said, walking up behind the pair. "Not right now."

His words had a calming effect on the big man, who looked up and nodded. "You're right."

. Abby, Kate, and Jack walked up to them, as once again the two groups separated into their original numbers.

"We need to keep moving, guys," Dwayne spoke, moving toward the second group.

"Yeah, it's going to be getting dark soon, and we will need to find some shelter," Sam added as she moved beside Dwayne. "We need to rest up, and maybe find some food too."

"Who made her queen bitch?" Leah asked under her breath.

"Leah, we would be dead if it wasn't for them," Ian replied, keeping his words even quieter.

"You don't know that. They probably just got lucky," Ronnie said, staring at the group.

He caught the unwanted attention of Jared, who had remained silent since they left the house. He made no attempt to interact but hung close to the group he belonged to. Nobody questioned him. They could all feel there was something about him, and while nobody could say for sure what it was, they knew better than to push him for fear of the result.

"Well, they have gotten us this far, maybe we should just let them lead," Abby suggested, her voice meek. Even though they had been elevated into the same ranks as Ian, Ronnie, and Leah, the fact remained that the trio did not belong with them.

"What would you know about it?" Leah snapped, her works snarky and barbed.

Abby lowered her eyes to the ground and took a step back, her deep shuddering breath said she was on the verge of tears.

"Guys, we need to move, now," Sam growled at them, pointing down the road to a group of at least half a dozen zeds making their way toward them.

The group moved, the two divisions joining up once again as they walked. Three things dominated the outskirt of the city: parks, small rows of housing and tenement blocks, and industrial zones. The silence of the city only hit them once they approached the factory site. The canned goods factory worked day and night, and while the noise was contained behind the reinforced building, there was always a general undertone of sound that buzzed around it. Even on cold, winter days when ninety percent were locked up indoors, clinging to their heating units, or the early mornings when the world still seemed to be asleep, there was always a hum about the place. The very fact people were alive and surrounding each other, created a sort of white noise that played out on a subconscious level.

Now it was gone, stripped away by the returning dead. The only real sounds were their hungry growls, and while they echoed up and down the streets, like a snarling winter wind, they carried no sense of warmth or life. Merely an exclamation point at the end of the silence.

"Which way?" Ian asked, looking to Sam for answers.

While none wanted to readily admit it, Ian understood that a leader was required, and real-world situations called for real leaders, not the winner of the popularity contest.

"If we cut through the park, we would come to the downtown district. There would be plenty of places to hide," Ronnie offered.

Jared gave a tisk of amused irritation.

"No," Sam answered quickly, deflecting the anger that instantly welled in Ronnie's eyes. "We can't go through the park. We would be too exposed."

"Plus, we want to leave the city," Dwayne added. "Not move further into it. There are lots of people around here still, mostly dead, some alive, but we are best to stick together. We don't know who we can trust."

"Well, unless you want to hide in the factory, we are running out of options," Jack spoke up, his song-like voice weak and timid, yet his eyes burned with a serious intensity.

The others looked over their shoulders and saw a mob of the undead stumbling around at the other end of the road. They came around a city bus, which had been parked sideways across the road.

"Shit," Julie said, staring down at the group. "There has to be at least fifty of them, maybe more."

The horde of zeds did not appear to have noticed the group yet. But with each shuffling step they took, the distance between them decreased, and so the less time they had before things changed.

"We can hide out in the factory. It's huge, and I know for a fact the industry is dying. They were laying people off left, right, and center;

running on a skeleton crew," Jack said, pushing his broken glasses up his nose.

"How can you be so sure?" Ronnie snapped, throwing a glance back in Jack's direction.

"Because my old man used to work there. They laid him off a month or so ago, after thirty years of working there." The bitterness in his voice overpowered the fear.

The news seemed to come as a shock to Abby, and while nobody truly knew the extent of their relationship, to say that they were close was a simple fact to tell.

"How many people is a graveyard shift?" Ronnie asked.

"I dunno, but it can't be many, and at least inside there are places to hide. Out here, we are sitting ducks," Jack said, sweat sliding down his greasy brow.

"I still vote for through the park," Ronnie said, looking up at the tall, grey structure that was the factory. Thick steel pipes wrapped their way around the building like snakes, while trucks sat in their bays, waiting for their cargo to be delivered.

They would be waiting a long time.

"You would because you're an asshole," Jared sniped again, his words few but barbed and laced with enough venom to piss off even the most patient man.

"What the fuck did you say to me?" Ronnie charged at Jared, throwing Jack to one side as he stormed past him.

Turning toward the charging jock, Jared didn't flinch, and made no move to fight, yet.

"Hey ... hey, stop it," Julie said, moving between the two men. Samantha joined her, and the pair managed to slow Ronnie down enough for Leah to grab his arms and pull him away.

"You need to watch your words, cocksucker, because I'll close that mouth for you permanently if you don't," Ronnie spat as his face turned red with a deep-seated and bubbling rage.

"Yeah, I'd like to see you try," Jared said, garnering a stern look from both Julie and Sam.

"Just cut it out," Julie said, walking up to Jared in an attempt to lead him away from the confrontation.

"This way," Dwayne called up to them. He had broken away from the group, making his way down the slope to the edge of the cannery compound. "We can shimmy over this."

As if a demonstration was needed, he hurried up the chain-link fence, flipping over the top to land gently on the other side.

"I'll never be able to do that." Jack panted as he reached the bottom of the slope.

"Well, it was your idea, genius, so you'd better learn." Ronnie was in a foul mood, and ready to react to anybody that spoke.

Sam and Jared were over the wall before anybody really even heard them go. The rattle of the fence drew the attention of the dead inside the compound, but they had enough time to get everybody over and into the factory … if everybody moved fast.

Julie and Leah went next. Both ladies struggled but made it up and over the fence in decent time. Ronnie stood back, being oddly courteous in making sure the two remaining women of the group made it to safety.

Ian surprised everybody with how quick he made it up and over, while Abby and Kate made easy work of the climb up, although both seemed somewhat timid on the descent.

"See you on the other side, man," Ronnie spoke to Jack, clapping him on the shoulder. "You can do this."

Ronnie was over the fence and down the other side like a cat. He hardly made a sound at all as he completed his climb.

"Come on, Jack," Abby urged, her eyes pleading with her best friend to make the move.

Grabbing the fence, Jack tried to heave himself from the ground four times before finally succeeding. The fence rattled and reverberated across its length, like a deathly round of applause.

Jack clung on for dear life as he reached the top. Swinging one leg over he stopped, straddling the fence as if it were three hundred feet in the air and there was nothing below him but a long drop down to a rocky demise.

"You're almost there," Abby offered her encouragement. "Just let go."

The drop was more than ten feet, and so while letting go was the only option, it was one that made Jack pause for thought. The landing would hurt, but it would get Jack down from the fence. He couldn't do it, however. His leg was stuck and he could not bring it up and over without losing his balance.

A sound from the other side startled them. The first group of zeds had arrived and were sliding down the embankment toward the compound. Unable to control their descent, the sudden change in pitch sent them all toppling down, not stopping until they impacted against the fence.

One came to rest with a jarring snap of breaking bones. One look at the way its shoulder rose with such prominence under its checkered work shirt was enough to confirm the injury.

"Hurry up, we don't have much time," Sam spoke up, as she eyed the group of zeds coming their way from around the trucks.

"I'm trying," Jack said, as his death grip on the fence intensified.

"Oh, for fuck sake!" Jared growled.

Jumping up, he grabbed hold of Jack's leg and hauled him over and down. Jack let out an agonized howl as he fell, his leg catching on the sharpened points that lined the fence. Blood stained his trousers a much darker shade as he lay whimpering on the floor.

"Can we go now?" Jared eyeballed the group, challenging them to say something against him.

When nobody said anything, he turned and walked away.

"What the hell has crawled into his butt?" Sam asked Julie once Jared had moved out of immediate earshot.

"It's this place," Julie answered. "This world now. He thinks he has to be a hard ass to survive … I think."

Whatever it was, everybody was starting to get an understanding for Jared, and while he was useful to have around, he was not working his way into their graces as being a core confidant.

The main compound around the factory was made up of three areas. A carpark for the staff and a separate section for any visitors who felt a day excursion to a canning factory was a fun way to pass the time. There were also the truck bays, which were occupied by trucks and rigs without their rear compartments.

"This place carried on working right until the end," Samantha said in a tone of near awe as the group headed toward the building.

The five zeds that had appeared around the trucks were gaining on them. Their snarls close enough to make the hairs on Julie's arms stand erect.

"Come on, we can get in here," Dwayne said, pointing ahead to an open cargo door. "Quickly, we can't hold them off."

The group hurried over, with Jack limping behind them, Abby by his side the entire time.

The cargo bay was about five feet in the air, and so Dwayne dropped down and turned to face the group.

"I'll give you a boost," he said, looking at Samantha, who had rapidly become his cohort in the world. "Any sign of trouble and you bail. We will find something else."

Samantha nodded at him as she stepped into his cupped hands. With a slight push, Dwayne hoisted her up and onto the platform.

Sam disappeared inside, coming back a few moments later with the all clear.

"Hurry," Dwayne said, holding his hands for Julie and Kate to head up next. Ronnie was straight behind them, still clutching his blood-encrusted crowbar. It clanged when he dropped it on the metal grating as he hauled himself up and into the loading bay.

"Way to go," Jared said as he walked up to Dwayne.

"Dude, just give him a break. He's a cool guy, and we are in this together," Dwayne whispered as Jared stepped into him.

"I know. That's the fucking problem. Too many people will slow us down," Jared answered.

His eyes were cold and his words even colder. To the point it made Dwayne shiver, and the lingering presence of Jared's boot in his hands made him feel as if a ghost had passed through him.

Dwayne had never had any reason to fear a living person before, but being around Jared, he was starting to get the feeling there were a lot worse things out there than the zeds wandering around.

The dead had closed the gap, their snarls echoing around the trucks like a howling wind.

"Hurry," Dwayne urged.

Ian stepped in, up, and over, disappearing into the factory. He moved with the skill of someone who knew what they were doing. Dwayne saw this and made a note to try to get chatting with the man away from the others.

Abby looked back at Jack, and for a moment froze, but Dwayne grabbed her foot and hauled her up. She scrambled and disappeared, only for her face to reappear over the ledge.

"Listen, you've got this, dude. You saved us by bringing us here. Now, come on, let's carry on being safe," Dwayne whispered to Jack, before offering him a fist bump. Jack smiled and then a look of grim determination hit his face. "Atta boy!"

Pushing hard, Dwayne heaved Jack up to the bay, holding him as he swung himself up in a cumbersome fashion. Both his extra weight and crippling fear working to slow him down.

The dead were close. Dwayne turned to jump up to the others. Crouching, he launched himself, caught the edge, and pulled himself up. He swung his legs up onto the loading dock and stood, off balance but secure, on the edge of the bay.

Stepping away he looked back and stared into the black eyes of the dead. The group of seven zeds pushed and shoved against the edge of the bay, but none showed the level of thought needed to climb up to get to their prey.

Turning, Dwayne moved inside to the others.

The factory looked deserted, although none of them allowed themselves the luxury of entertaining the idea that they were lucky enough for that to happen.

The machinery was powered down, but the echoing growls of the undead made it feel as if it was still a hub of activity. It was a comfort they found solace in. A little background noise to their otherwise silent world. For a few moments they felt as if they were safe. Nothing more than a group of students on a field trip.

Then the first of the dead began to emerge. Two zeds appeared from behind a triple-stacked pallet of canned goods. Both wore the same company uniform. One was missing a good portion of his throat, which caused its head to sit on an inquisitive angle upon its shoulders. The other walked with a pronounced limp; a bloody tear in the flank of his overalls showed the bite marks that had sealed his fate.

"We need to move," Dwayne said, turning to lead them away. "Jack, which way?"

Jack looked at Dwayne for a second before responding, speaking just as it felt he would not offer anything of use.

"The main work floor is through here. I don't know it well enough, but we can move this way," Jack said, his voice sounding stronger now that he was back on the ground.

Dwayne moved beside him, leading the way. "You've got this. Bring us someplace safe."

Jack led the way hoping he didn't lead them into trouble. The others followed, huddled together, with Ronnie holding his crowbar at the ready. Abby and Kate both had kitchen knives, but they had tucked them into their trousers like pirates.

Dwayne was armed with a long metal pipe, while Samantha had a baseball bat. The aluminum weapon was dented and smeared with the blood of her enemies; scarred with the lives it had claimed like any great weapon should be.

The main factory floor was a cramped affair, with plenty of fresh dead waiting for a meal to walk their way. The majority were trapped behind their stations at the various points of the conveyer-belt line, and like their simple-minded brethren outside, lacked the mental fortitude to climb over or under the objects in question.

One man, a tall, black-skinned fellow with bloodshot eyes, leaned over and made a grab at Abby, but Ronnie responded by caving in the side of the dead man's skull with his crowbar. The sound of shattering bone was weak, cushioned by the squishing sound of scrambled brain matter.

The creature fell forward onto the belt, fluids leaking from the gaping hole in its skull.

"Thanks," Abby said, breathless.

"We need to keep moving." The word came from the front, hurrying them along.

The factory floor was not the easiest to navigate. With its myriad of conveyor belts, it looked like an industrial themed queue for a *Disneyland* ride. They snaked their way through, ducking under the belts and rigging, while above their heads a maze of metal piping and valves watched on. Each one brought a specific ingredient to a specific vat or section of the process.

"The canteen is this way; the offices are at the back and upstairs. The reception is through there, after the locker rooms and storage units. It's a long corridor, and probably full of people," Jack said.

"Why do you think that?" Sam asked, looking around trying to decide which direction she preferred.

"I was here with Dad once when the fire alarm went off. Everybody left and gathered through there. Now, they were laying the ground crew off, but the offices were still manned, and anybody here would either go out the back where we came in, or through those doors there." Jack pointed straight away at a set of double doors hidden by strips of plastic that dangled from the roof like curtains.

"We can head upstairs, find a place to lay low, buy us some time to plan our next move," Dwayne offered, looking around to give people the chance to object.

"Or we head for some food in the canteen," Samantha said.

"Food sounds good," Ronnie agreed.

"I'm thirsty," Abby said.

"What if it is full of ... them?" Leah said, holding Ronnie's hand as she spoke, squeezing it at the mere mention of the undead.

"She's got a point. The canteen was pretty much always open," Jack offered, looking around, his sweat-sheened face beginning to pale as the adrenaline wore off.

"I think the office idea sounds good to me," Ian said, speaking for the first time since they hopped the fence.

"We should keep moving," Jared said, once again economical with his words but managing to convey volumes with his tone alone.

"Where are we going to go? We need a plan," Sam asked.

"We have a plan. Keep moving. If we stop, we die," Jared said, eyeballing Sam, who would not allow herself to be intimidated.

"Really, you think stopping to rest is going to get us killed, even if we find a secure place upstairs." She folded her arms across her chest.

"We need to make a decision guys, like yesterday," Ronnie said as he walked away from the group to put down an approaching zed. The hairnet covering the top of their skull turned a rusty brown by the time the creature hit the floor.

"What's the quickest way out?" Dwayne asked, looking to Jack.

"Uh … through those doors." He pointed. "Straight down the corridor, then there are several side hallways that lead to emergency exits. I used them for smoking."

Everybody in the group looked at him.

"Fine. I used to work here during the summer, also, to get enough to help pay for school," he admitted, explaining his knowledge of the factory layout.

Dwayne eyeballed the doors and moved forward slowly. Pulling back the plastic curtains, he froze. "Looks like we are going upstairs," he said, matter-of-factly.

"Why, what is it?" Kate asked, fear overpowering her.

"Well, these guys took precautions to keep whatever was on the other side of this door away from them." Dwayne stepped to one side and showed everybody the thick chain linking tied around the door handles, effectively locking them in.

"Shit. What if we can't get out?" Abby asked, her voice panicked.

Behind them, death snarled as several sets of gnashing teeth snapped at them.

"Shit," Leah cried out, jumping out of the way of a killer hug aimed in her direction.

Samantha stepped forward, swinging her bat as if she were intending to knock the stitches out of the ball. She connected with the side of a dead woman's face, caving in her cheekbones and knocking her to the floor. The next swipe was a vertical one that came crashing down on the bald head of an older man with a pronounced chin. The result of the strike left his head looking oddly heart shaped and dropped him to the floor. Both were still alive, although the man was more spasms than any real purposeful forward motion.

"Come on, hurry," Dwayne called, ushering the group toward the wrought iron staircase leading to the second floor. Their footsteps echoed as they made their way up, their new lofty position seeming to agitate the gathered crowd below. Somewhere, something crashed, sending a long rolling rumble through the building.

"What was that?" Leah cried out.

"No idea, but let's keep moving," Dwayne spoke from the front.

"It sounds like a rumbling stomach," Abby said

"The factory wants to eat us," Kate said, her voice cold and serious.

They followed Jack through the factory. While the ground floor was divided into different segments, the upper floor, with its offices and meeting rooms, formed more of a perimeter. The single corridor ran the entire length, with rooms spawning from it at regular intervals. Each one was labeled, and most were empty if the view afforded in the many different windows were any indication.

"Why don't we just stop here?" Julie asked as they walk alongside a boardroom. The long table had seats for a dozen or so people, and a giant television screen hung on the far wall, consuming almost the entire area.

"We should head to the main office," Jack said, his focus on the destination.

"You heard the man," Dwayne offered his support before anybody had the chance to voice a different opinion.

The main management office was an open and luxurious space. A small area had been created for a receptionist in a hallway office before the real space began. The floor was carpeted a deep red color, while floor to ceiling windows ran along the far wall. There were no drapes on the inside, but electronic blinds were positioned on the outside. Two of the five windows were shaded, while the others were open. The daylight streamed in, making the office seem that much more spacious. A messy desk stood to the left at the far end of the room, and filing cabinets lined the wall. A table with three chairs stood on the other side with plenty of empty space in between.

"Someone had delusions of grandeur," Samantha said as she peered around the office.

"Tacky and cheap," Jack said. "Just like the guy who worked here."

The words brought a snigger from Abby and Kate, who seemed to be more in tune with Jack than any of the others.

"Where to now?" Dwayne asked, just as another crash boomed through the building.

There was an unmistakable quality to the rumble none of them failed to understand. The building shook, as if it too were terrified of what was happening, as the din reverberated through the factory, drowned out by the next crash before it had the chance to finish its journey.

"We're not alone here," Ronnie said.

"Wow, I'll take stating the fucking obvious for five hundred, Alex," Jared snapped.

He had moved to the window behind the manager's desk. It afforded him a view of the front entrance of the factory. Two four-by-fours and a truck were parked outside. A group of around a dozen heavily armed people stood milling around, watching something.

Another loud crash came, although this one had a higher pitch and a less hollow ring to it; it was a more permanent sound.

"They are in," Dwayne said, not needing to look out of the window to confirm his statement.

"They mean business too," Jared said, watching as half the waiting group disappeared from view.

A few moments later, the rattle of automatic gunfire roared through the factory.

"What do they want?"

"Who are they?"

"What are we going to do?' Leah, Abby, and Kate all asked at the same time, their words overrunning one another, making it impossible to decipher who really asked what.

"We need to move," Dwayne said, turning back to the group. "We can't stay here."

"Then where do you expect us to go?" Kate snapped, the stress of the day taking its toll on her.

"Anywhere is better than here," Ian offered in response, once again putting himself in between people as a calm-headed mediator.

"Maybe not," Jack spoke up.

"How do you mean?" Sam asked.

"Yeah, dude, these guys are armed and mean business." Dwayne joined in the conversation.

"Yes, but they are not after us. They don't even know we are here. My bet is they are after the warehouse. You know, looking for supplies. If we lay low here, they will be in and out without even knowing about us." Jack looked around the group, skipping Jared, not that it was a noticeable jump, as he had moved from the window to join the others.

"He's got a point," Jared admitted, almost begrudgingly. "Besides, there is at least a dozen of them, with three cars. They will run us down if we try to make it out."

The news made Kate whimper and brought Abby to her side. Stroking her friend's hair, Abby pulled Kate close against her, trying to quieten her sobs.

"It's your call, Chief," Ian addressed Dwayne but looked at both he and Samantha.

The pair stared at one another as if weighing up the responsibility that had not officially been bestowed upon them.

"Go lock the door." Dwayne glanced at Jared, who moved off without offering any snarky comments.

"Try to close the blinds too," Sam added. "The rest of you, get down on the floor over here by the desk. They can't see this far into the office."

Everybody moved slowly, terrified of making a sound that may bring trouble to their door.

"Stay down low," Dwayne whispered as another burst of gunfire rang out. Closer this time, it made everything seem that much more real.

"They are shooting the dead. Maybe they will help us," Leah offered, throwing out a different opinion on their predicament.

"These guys don't seem like the introductions type. They would shoot us the moment they saw us," Dwayne answered, speaking with a certainty he could not explain.

"You don't know that," Leah said.

"Are you willing to risk it?" Sam added, staring at Leah, who squirmed under her gaze.

Leah didn't answer. Instead, she shrank down onto the floor, pressing herself against the wall, her knees pulled up to her chest.

"So, what ... we just wait it out?" Ronnie asked, impatient. His irritation at Dwayne and the others in his group grew with each passing moment.

"I guess," Julie said. She shuffled to one side as Jared rejoined them, the atmosphere becoming a bit more awkward because of his presence.

"Just a thought." Ian paused, his facial expression saying he wished to take back the sentence he had started.

"What?" Kate asked, her tears had subsided. She sat beside Abby, their fingers interlocked, her thumb stroking the back of her friend's hand.

"It's nothing." Ian tried to back out of it.

"Spill, rich boy," Jared snarled.

"Fuck you, you loner prick," Ronnie growled, unable to contain himself any longer.

Everything happened in a rush. Nobody knew who moved first, but before anybody could react, Ronnie and Jared were locked in a tussle.

To look at, it was a mismatch all the way. Ronnie was taller, wider, and generally larger than Jared, yet when it came to a fight, the result was as one-sided as it got, in Jared's favor.

Jared ducked Ronnie's blows and delivered several shots of his own, including an elbow that broke Ronnie's nose with an audible pop of snapping cartilage. Ronnie dropped down low and drove his shoulder forward into Jared's gut, lifting him from the floor, only to hurl him backward, sending them crashing into the filing cabinets, creating a cacophonous din that surely announced their presence to anyone nearby.

Pushing off from the cabinets, Jared slipped from Ronnie's grip, driving his elbow down into the jock's trap muscle. Ronnie dropped, and before anybody saw it happen, Jared had pulled a serrated-edged knife from under his jacket and held it to Ronnie's throat.

The sharp blade rested against his flesh, pressing not hard enough to draw blood, but enough to leave a mark from its presence.

"Just give me a reason, fucktard," Jared panted.

Ronnie said nothing. His mouth hung open as he tried to suck in oxygen and his nose continued to pour blood down into his mouth, staining the blade a rich crimson.

Abby mistook the nasal blood for something else, and screamed, certain Ronnie's throat had been sliced. She collapsed to the floor in a faint and was caught by Jack who reacted just in time to stop her head from colliding with the corner of an overturned filing cabinet.

Leah found herself caught in the same misconception as Abby, and turned to empty her stomach over the floor, showering the wall in a chunky spray of sour-smelling vomit.

"Jared, dude, put that thing away," Dwayne spoke, holding his hands out and open toward the feuding pair.

"This pile of fuck started it." Jared sneered, turning to look at Ronnie, a flare of utter contempt flashing in his eyes.

"Well, you clearly ended it. Now put that thing away," Dwayne said, trying hard to defuse the situation before it spiraled any further out of control.

"These jock bastards are all the same. Think they own the world, but introduce them to the real world and they are all pussies." The emotion in Jared's voice flowed on a river of anger, pouring from a source far more deep-seated than his recent relationship with Ronnie.

"Guys," Sam tried to shush them, but a crash against the office door interrupted her.

Julie screamed—an instinctive reaction—as she jumped backward almost into Ian's arms.

"We hear you in there," a gruff voice sounded. "Come out and nobody needs to get hurt."

"Yeah, right," Jared offered, the knife still pressed against Ronnie's throat.

"What do we do?" Julie asked, looking around frantically from person to person.

Jack moved first, surprising everybody. "Fire escape, by the window behind the desk."

A crash against the door got everybody moving.

"It won't hold them long," Samantha said, watching as Dwayne followed Jack to the escape.

"I won't ask you again. Come out and nobody has to get hurt," the voice on the other side of the door yelled.

"I really don't believe him," Julie said.

"Come on, quickly." Dwayne had opened the window and studied the escape route.

The metal staircase took them down to the ground but put them directly in range of the group waiting outside. The freshly re-dead corpses that dotted the ground told them any sign of movement and the cavalry would shoot, regardless of any possible, albeit thin, good intentions.

"We go up," Jack spoke again, his sudden rush of good ideas not stopping yet.

"To the roof?" Dwayne asked as if that detail needed to be confirmed.

"Makes more sense than going down. We can hide up there, and maybe we will get lucky and they leave us alone."

"Sounds like a plan to me." Dwayne turned to the group, who had been watching their conversation with eager eyes. "Go. One at a time."

He was relieved to see Jared had lowered his knife, but the uneasy feeling that had a hold over his gut told him the issue was far from resolved. While he did not know Jared overly well, he now understood there was a much darker side to him than just being a slight social outcast.

It was not a box he wanted to open, not at that point in time, and if pushed for honesty, not ever. Jared was a cool guy, but they did not need someone like that in the group.

Or do you? The voice echoed in Dwayne's head as Jared passed him without so much as a nod or even a glance.

Another crash at the door and the wood splintered. Not enough to give way, but enough to bring a second and third crash in quick succession.

"Kate, hurry," Abby called, as she reached the window and cast a final glance back into the office.

"Go, I'll get her," Dwayne said, all but shoving the scared young woman out of the window.

"Kate, please," Abby cried, moving through the window, holding on as long as possible before disappearing.

"Kate, come on, you can do this," Dwayne encouraged, holding his hand out as a means of shortening the distance Kate had to travel alone.

She moved a short way, her steps slow and tentative as if walking a tightrope above a sheer drop onto rock ground far below. Suddenly, her eyes went wide and her head snapped backward. Kate was hauled from her feet, and it took a fraction of a second longer than it should for Dwayne to understand what had happened.

An arm burst through the door, the skin rippling with muscle, making the tattoos that covered its every inch dance as if they were alive and calling the shots.

Someone had grabbed hold of Kate's long blond hair and pulled back hard.

Screaming, Kate stumbled backward, and Dwayne moved to grab her.

"Run," she whispered as she flailed backward.

"I've got you now, honey," the voice snarled as the hand released her hair, only for a forearm to slide under her chin. It gave her assailant the chance to pull her against the door with enough force to further splinter the damaged wood.

Dwayne rushed forward, but he was too late. Kate was yanked back with such force that she disappeared through the door. The splintering wood tore deep gouges through her flesh as she was roughly yanked through a hole far too small.

Reversing his direction, Dwayne stumbled back and leaped out of the window onto the fire escape. He closed the exit point and hurried up to the roof, hauling himself over the ledge, before collapsing in a tired heap.

"Where's Kate?" Abby cried out.

Dwayne raised his head to respond, but Jack reacted the quickest and pulled Abby against him, stifling her cries.

"Shh, they can't find us," Jack implored, understanding that sometimes self-preservation was the only way to go. "Abby, Abby, listen to me. It's going to be all right."

Abby struggled against Jack's grip, breaking free from his hold. Her eyes were wild, her face twisted by grief into something feral and ugly. Turning around and searching for Dwayne, the target of her rage, she prepared to yell, only to be silenced when Jared appeared, his hand sliding over her mouth and his knife coming up before her eyes.

"Shut the fuck up if you want to carry on breathing," he growled.

Dwayne said nothing but watched on as Abby instantly calmed.

"Everybody get down, find something to hide behind, but for the love of God, don't make any noise," Samantha said, looking around at the terrified faces staring at her.

People moved slowly as if treading on eggshells, and if even one was to break, they would all be cast out and into a pit of fire. Moving in a crouch, she followed Dwayne over to the edge of the roof, not daring to lean across. The pipes that rose from the roof around them provided enough cover for them to hide without moving too far.

The others had similar ideas, and while they were not bunched together, the entire group hid among the same stretch of piping.

The group stood, frozen in fear, hidden, their melee style weapons were no match for the guns the other group possessed. All apart from Jared, who held his knife at the ready, looking every bit the crazy hunter.

"What ..." Leah whispered, her voice barely louder than the thundering of her heart.

She did not get to finish her thought because a hand clamped over her mouth. Offering no resistance, she looked over at Ian, who only removed his hand after she nodded the silent promise she would not say another word.

Time slowed, and the clouds above them drifted by far too quickly, while everything else seemed frozen. Like watching a movie where the subtitles are not quite in sync with the show; everything felt off to them.

Jared reacted first, unable to hold his position any longer. Inching his way along the pipes, he advanced with a strangely feline grace, his knife at the ready. He nodded at Dwayne as he passed, and the group's leader made no attempt to stop him.

The crash from below them shattered the silence, while the scream that accompanied it froze the blood in their veins.

"We've got a live one here," the same gruff voice spoke from down on the ground as had broken through the office door.

"Let me go, please." Kate's pleas drifted up to them, sounding all the more helpless after traveling the distance from her mouth to their ears.

Abby edged to the side of the roof and peered over. Dwayne made the same move but indicated for the others to remain where they were. Sliding over beside Abby, Dwayne readied himself to do whatever was necessary in order to protect the rest of the group.

Peering over the edge, they saw the three vehicles, all parked with the engines running. Four men stood outside, one against each four-by-four, and two against the open rear doors of the panel van. They were all armed with automatic rifles. The two by the van stood with theirs slung over their shoulders, their barrel chests puffed out as if they were guarding the most prized assets in the world, rather than a rusted-up, broken-down old Ford.

Across from the four men, forming a rough circle, were six others, again, each one was armed. Most held their guns ready, while one held a baseball bat in his hands, holding it the same way the others held their guns. His long blond hair flowed over his shoulders, and even from a distance, Dwayne could read the malicious intent in his eyes.

"Ain't she pretty," the blond man sneered, taking a step closer to Kate, who had been forced to her knees.

"Eli, take it easy," the tattooed man who had ripped Kate through the door spoke. He was not overly tall, but even from behind it was clear he was solidly built. He held his weapon in one hand and waggled a finger from the other toward his long-haired cohort. "We don't want to scare the poor thing … too early."

The man laughed, and the rest of the group joined in, cackling like a group of hyenas.

"How many others are in there?" an older man with grey hair and a thick, neatly trimmed beard asked.

"She said she is alone, that her old man worked here, and she came looking for him," the tattooed man answered, looking at the older man.

"You believed her?" the old man questioned.

For a moment, Dwayne wondered if he were wrong. If maybe the older man was the one in charge. His voice sounded far more prone to reason than his angry, tatted up friend. His faint hope died when the tattooed man walked over to the older member of the group and hit him in the stomach with the butt of his rifle. The sound of the man's breath leaving his body was clear even from the rooftop.

"Don't you ever question me, Leo," tattoo man growled.

Leo dropped down to a knee, snatching shallow, rattling breaths. Coughing and spitting the sudden torrent of saliva from his mouth, it looked as if he were doing everything in his power to prevent vomiting.

"I checked the room she was in. I saw nothing. Besides, you think a group would be dumb enough to hold up in a place like this? Fuck no," tattoo man continued.

"A group of bitches, maybe," one of the van guards spoke, bringing a round of laughter from everybody.

"Maybe, but then the rest wouldn't have been smart enough to hide from me, would they? Women can't think like that." Tattoo man took over the conversation once more.

"Shame, really. This one is pretty, but all on her lonesome, she's gonna spoil fast," the other van guard said, running his hands over his bloated belly.

Another round of laughter came from the ground, while beside him, Dwayne felt Abby tense. Reaching out, he placed a hand on her shoulder. He could feel her body, rigid beneath her clothes.

Abby looked over at him, and Dwayne shook his head. Now was not the time. Abby's eyes were red with tears, but she nodded in return. The tears fell, as she realized what she had just agreed to. Kate was lost to her, to all of them.

"You like sucking cock?" another of the armed guards spoke, bending down to get right in Kate's face.

"Fuck you." Kate's voice rose from the ground, finding its defiance when she needed it the most.

"Oh, oh, she's got a real dirty mouth on her. Good thing my cum will wash it clean, you useless slut," the man roared, grabbing hold of Kate's face with one hand. "How about I teach you a lesson right now. Bitches ain't good for talking. Fucking and cooking, that's what you get. Now, I don't see an oven around here, so you had better prove yourself useful in some other way."

"Go to hell," Kate growled, fear heavy on her words.

The man stood for a moment and looked down at her, nodding his head, as if lost in some deep level of contemplation.

He struck out with a roar, his fist crashing into the side of Kate's head, sending her to the floor. His roar became a cackled laugh as he danced around her fallen frame.

"Did you hear her? Did you, Billy?" He stopped and looked at tattoo man. "She needs to learn."

"Aye, that she does," tattoo man, whose real name of Billy was far too disappointing for such a vicious-looking man.

"You hear that, girly? You need to be taught a lesson, and Ed here is going to be the one to teach it." The man pointed at himself as he grabbed Kate's head and hauled her from the floor. "No, stay on your knees."

The order was followed by the jingle of a belt being loosened.

"No, please," Kate sobbed, her words almost inaudible through her cries.

"You keep moving those lips like that, and you gonna be saying yes a lot more often." Ed laughed.

Dwayne took ahold of Abby and pulled her over to him. He needed to use all his strength to do it.

"You don't want to watch this," he whispered, holding her tightly against him.

Her body was stiff, she lay against him straight, as if her joints had locked. Yet, she shook, with a tremor that grew and grew.

Dwayne sat with his back tight against the side wall of the factory roof and stared at the others, who were still hidden amongst the pipes.

Below them, Kate's cries were replaced by a wet, gagging sound that none of them needed to see to understand.

"Sweet Jesus, she's a natural. That's right, take it all, you little fuck on legs." Ed's words turned to hooted brays of delight.

On the roof, Abby's hands clenched against Dwayne, squeezing him with a strength harder than he realized a human could muster. Burying her face into his chest, Abby cried and bit down on her anguish so hard her teeth broke the skin of her bottom lip.

She thrashed and kicked against Dwayne's strong embrace as he fought to offer some comfort when she needed it the most.

Without warning, the group on the ground started laughing then yelling as Kate's mouth was finally freed up. The moment of silence that preceded her fresh wave of agonized screams was all the group needed to hear to fully understand what was happening below.

As Kate screamed and cried out, first in pain, and then, against all her self-control, in pure, albeit forced bliss, the others stood and crouched in frozen silence, forever haunted by the echo of abuse that would linger in their heads every time they closed their eyes from then through into eternity.

All the while Dwayne held Abby, his eyes were locked on Samantha, whose own eyes were stained bright red with tears. Her gaze screamed to him, telling him everything he needed to know about her past and the thing that had happened to her. Back in the world before it officially went to hell, back when they lived in a world filled with denial. A world that was dying long before the dead came to reclaim it as their own.

The assault seemed to last an age, and when the cries finally fell still, Dwayne found himself hoping Kate was dead.

Rage built up inside him as he fought the urge to run down and launch himself at the men. Unarmed and just a boy compared to them, he knew it was a fool's errand, but it was a consuming notion, nonetheless.

He saw the same look on Jared's face. He did not know what to make of the man he had spent so much time cooped up with since the change. But he did know that he would not turn him away. The attack hardened him and forced him to understand that the world was not the same place it had been, the survivors no longer had to play by the same rules as before, and that knowledge changed everything. Jared could well be a killer, or maybe even a complete psychopath, but if that was what it took to make their group strong and stop anybody else from being taken, then he was willing to pay the price.

"Get her in the truck," Ed's voice finally spoke. Out of breath, and proud as a fucking rooster, he gave the orders and walked away.

Dwayne chanced a look over his shoulder as one of the group hauled a limp Kate from the ground and hurled her into the back of the left-hand four-by-four. He saw Ed get into the passenger side of the same car. His eyes narrowed, memorizing the license plate, the same way he memorized the cold, sharp-pointed features of the man called Ed. The black hair, thinning on the top, and the ratty goatee that clung to his face without any real conviction.

It was not much to go on, but Dwayne made himself a promise, a silent one to the group, that he would find that man and kill him. He would track him down, and regardless of what hands fate dealt the man, be it the leader of the new world, or a bum on the street with his last breaths already filling his infected lungs, Dwayne would cut his heart out and grind it beneath his boot.

The assault could not have lasted more than a few minutes. It felt like an age to the group trapped on the roof, but with all of the zeds arounds, any fun and games on the ground would have to have been enjoyed quickly. A burst of gunfire told the tale of the route they took, and a while later the heavy metallic clangs of a trolley rolled up to the vans.

Chancing another glance, Dwayne watched as the two larger members of the unit began to load the pallets of supplies into the back of their van. With the job done, the others got into their cars, and the group drove away.

They gave no sound as to their destination or future intentions.

Only once the echo of their engines had finally faded into nothing, did people feel strong enough to move. Coming together as a unit, they gathered around Dwayne, who held the now sleeping Abby in his arms like a parent cradling a sick child.

One by one, everybody huddled around the stricken girl.

"She's going into shock," Leah said, crouching down.

"I can't believe what's happening," Julie said, sliding down to sit beside Dwayne.

"We have to get her back." Ronnie stood, defiant, but his pale, sweat-drenched face said that he was just as shaken as the rest of them.

"Where do we go?" Samantha asked, crouching down to check Abby for a pulse.

"I don't know … I don't fucking know," Dwayne said, banging his head back against the wall.

Sitting there, he closed his eyes and tried to let his mind escape the swirling storm of torment that hung directly over their heads. It crept among them like a rolling fog, with tendrils reaching out to curl around their bodies, slowly overtaking them; choking and cloying, almost as if it were a physical thing.

"We will figure it out," Sam spoke softly, sitting beside Dwayne on his free side, she placed a hand on his shoulder.

He didn't give an answer. He didn't think he even had one.

"Do you really think this is what the world is like now?" Leah asked as she leaned against Ronnie.

Everybody was sitting on the roof, still adrift in the churning sea of emotions.

"I think they made it pretty clear," Jack said, his voice broken and despondent.

"Yeah, those assholes, but I mean the rest of it. The state, the US, fuck, I don't know, the rest of the world. Are the dead everywhere, and are the living really so dangerous?" Leah asked, desperate for some reassurance.

"I miss my mom," Julie whimpered as she drew her knees up to her chest and rested her head on them.

Silence fell over them, and as if to further dampen their mood, the clouds that had formed above their heads continued to darken, growing pregnant not only with rain but rather with a storm.

"I know people don't want to hear it, but those guys did do one thing for us," Jared said as he moved back toward the group from the other side of the factory roof.

"What is it?" Dwayne asked, looking up at the man that split his viewpoint so completely.

"They took down all of the zeds in the courtyard. I don't know about the factory, but we can get down to the ground from up here." Jared pointed to the other two fire escapes, which ran right down to the ground, and into the far courtyard.

"What are you getting at?" Sam asked, pushing the conversation along.

"Cars, trucks, vans, you name it, fuck, a frigging semi, if anybody could drive it. I'm talking about getting some wheels under our asses so that we can high-tail it out of here pronto." Jared smiled, proud of himself.

Before, back in the room above the non-stop student kegger, that smile had spoken a lot. It had comforted Julie and served as the icebreaker they all needed back when things first started going to hell.

Now, it had a strange quality, the earlier altercation between Jared and Ronnie, while seen coming from a mile away, had somehow tainted

Jared's smile. Leaving behind more a smear of what had once been than anything else.

"Where would we go?" Leah asked without even raising her head. "It's all hopeless, right?"

"We could get away from here. We could get ourselves some weapons and go after those fuckers that took her girl." Jared pointed at Abby, who was stirring in Dwayne's arms.

"Really, you think we can just drive in and ask for her back?" Ronnie said, his voice stripped of the confrontational tone that had been there since the moment they met.

"Why not?" Jared answered, holding Ronnie's fractured gaze with his own cold, cool stare. "We plan it out, strike at night and free her."

"They'll kill us before we even get close," Ian said. "Those guys knew what they were doing. I don't know about you, but I've never fired a gun, and I'm pretty sure nobody else here has either."

Everyone looked at each other. Only Dwayne and Samantha did not lower their heads.

"I fired a handgun at a range before," Dwayne said reluctantly. He was painfully aware of how pitiful that level of experience sounded, especially in light of their current situation.

"My old man is a cop," Samantha said. "I've fired a few guns, as he taught me to protect myself, but I don't own one, and, well, like Dwayne here, I've never fired outside of a range."

The first few drops of rain fell on the group. Fat beads of water fell so slowly, their path through the air could almost be traced.

One by one, they looked up as the heavens opened—as if the world itself was crying at their predicament.

Rain pelted down on them, soaking them to the skin in an instant.

The water shocked Abby back to life. Dwayne had the misfortune of seeing the confused haze lift from behind her eyes. He was forced to watch realization dawn on her, and to see her heart break again as she realized everything really did happen. It was not some dream.

"We can't stay out here," Leah called.

"Jared's right, we need to get mobile," Julie added, shouting to be heard above the pounding rain. Behind them, the main working section of the property was covered by metal roofing, which echoed the raindrops like rolling thunder.

"Let's get down and into something. Once we are out of the rain, we can decide," Samantha said, looking over at Dwayne for support.

He nodded, and Samantha held out her hand to help Abby to her feet.

"Come with me. There are a few choices over here." Jared led them back to the part of the roof he had been exploring.

One by one, they all followed him as the sky continued to darken, ushering in a false darkness over the world.

CHAPTER SIX

The damage to the perimeter fencing was not too severe, and after first removing the zed's leg, and then the razor wire from around it, they were able to carry out a suitable repair, which would hold up until they had the chance to finish their fortification plans.

"We should head back," Henry said, wiping sweat from his forehead.

Hector stood farther along the fence, checking for any secondary damage caused by the troublesome zed the day before.

"You go. I just want to finish checking this stretch. We are lucky that herd came in from the other side. Otherwise, they would have torn this thing apart, not to mention wandering right into the camp." Hector twisted the razor wire into place against a thick tree branch.

"Nope, nobody goes off alone. You know the rules, man," Henry said, insistent.

"This is hardly off camp. I can practically see the shelter from here," Hector argued, but Henry would not budge.

Looking around the woods, Henry took in the silence. Something felt different. He didn't know if it was because of the events of the day before, and getting caught in the middle of a herd, or what. The only thing he knew for certain was that something felt off. Something in his gut, telling him to be extra vigilant.

"We're heading back. My watch is about to start, it's almost chow time, and I want you and Taron to head out to the rear this afternoon and do some scouting."

"You mean fucking fruit picking," Hector shot back, clearly annoyed at the task he had been given. "I'd rather do a double shift in the lookout shelter."

"We're not doing doubles, not after last time," Henry answered fast, walking down along the fence toward Hector. "I want Taron to look for the fruit bushes. You can hunt whatever you want, so long as you stay together. You know the rules, man. Nobody goes out alone."

Hector remained silent, and it was clear something was bothering him, but he kept his mouth shut and followed orders. They had all elected Henry to lead the group, and deep down, Hector knew it was the right choice.

They made their way back to the camp just as the first jet plane roared overhead. The growl of its engines shook the ground they stood on, and tore through the trees, the rumbling echo destroying the silence of the area for miles around.

Three more jets appeared, flying in a loose formation that only saw two pass within their line of sight.

"What the hell was that?" Vanessa cried, running out of the lookout. Behind her, Taron and James appeared from the rear building, their eyes raised to the heavens.

Henry opened his mouth to speak, but explosions tore through the woods and had them all running for the shelter.

"Get in the shelter." Taron pushed James ahead of him as they sprinted for the safety of their bunker.

Henry was the first there as the second round of detonations added to the destructive din. Wrenching open the door, he stood outside, ushering his wife, son, and friends inside first before following them and closing the door.

"We rehearsed for this too," Hector called, taking over the role as leader as they had agreed. "We are under attack. We don't know what has happened, or if it is related to the zeds, so we treat this as the top-level threat. Everybody underground."

Working together, Hector and Taron lifted the double bed unit that Henry and Vanessa slept in. The hinges were stiff but they worked, exposing the hidden second level of the bunker. Designed as both a storage reserve and a shelter in case of extreme emergencies, it had enough supplies to keep the group alive for a month or two, if they were strict with their rations.

"Mommy, I don't want to," James whimpered, clinging to his mother's legs.

"I know, honey, but it is going to be fine. This is just a precaution. Come on, just like we practiced." Gently, Vanessa coaxed her son down into the bunker. Henry followed, with Hector and Taron close behind, lowering the bed back into place.

The bunker was cramped and with the canned goods stored there, the available space was further reduced.

"What do we do now?" Vanessa asked her husband, as she stroked James' hair.

The boy was hugging her leg as if his life depended on it, his eyes closed, sweat gleaming on his forehead.

"We lay low," Henry answered. "We have enough supplies down here to survive. We give it time to settle, and then Taron and I will head through the tunnel to see what damage has been caused."

"Did you see those jets?" Hector asked, whispering.

"No, it was too quick," Henry answered. "I was not really expecting it."

"Well, I did. Didn't think it was possible at first, but the second one confirmed it." He looked from Taron back to Henry again.

"Then spit it out," Taron pushed.

"They were American."

"They were ours?" Vanessa said, overhearing the conversation.

She had managed to distract James with some coloring pencils and a book of superheroes.

"Yep, I'm sure of it," Hector answered, his rotating gaze now also including a stop at Vanessa. "You know what that means, right?"

"Yeah," Henry answered, catching on to the point Hector was trying to make. "We are fighting back."

The tunnel was cramped and had only been built as a rudimentary fall back in case they needed to make a quick escape. There was, probably, just as much chance of it collapsing under any locational threat than of it letting them through alive, but life or death scenarios validated its creation.

Taron had the lead, with Henry right behind him. Taron held a flashlight in one hand, and a machete in the other, while Henry had a rifle over his shoulder, ready for any high-powered assault that may be required.

The tunnel opened up on the other side of the trees, through a self-constructed gateway. They had acquired the old sewer grating from a scrapyard several years before. Covered with crawling vines, it was well hidden by nature. The hinges groaned as they were forced to open. The initial cry caused Taron to jump back, fearful of drawing any additional attention.

"Just do it," Henry said, reassuring his friend.

They climbed out, instantly alert for any danger that may lurk. Once they were sure there were no wandering post-humans in the near vicinity, they allowed their attention to be turned to the devastation that lay on the horizon.

The city lay in ruins, broken and battered. Flames licked upward into the sky as if the ground had opened and the fires of hell had seeped out. The ground rumbled from the explosions, and even as they stood on the edge of the trees, the rush of wind from the initial detonations rolled over them.

Several taller buildings on what remained of the skyline collapsed, disappearing inward upon themselves, as if being claimed by the escaping damned.

"What is going on?" Vanessa asked as the jet planes turned back over the city, heading toward them.

One final round of explosions hit the city before the four jets turned and sped away, disappearing behind the glare of the sun.

"I think we are fighting back," Hector said, his voice sounding happy at the sight of such destruction.

"But I don't understand." Vanessa took hold of Henry's arm, using him as her anchor, to keep herself from falling.

"It makes sense," Taron said, his voice weak as if he did not want to speak the words.

"What does? Blowing innocent people up?" Vanessa held her hands over James' ears, pressing him close against her, hoping to drown out the sights and sounds of the new world from his child's mind.

"Think about it, V. The highest concentrations of post-humans are going to be in the cities. We came to that conclusion ourselves." Taron looked at her while the fires began to settle, dropping down to the ground level.

To those watching, it looked as if the fires sank back down into the ground, called back down to where they belonged.

"We also said that is because there will be a lot of survivors there too," Vanessa snapped.

"We are fighting a war. The cities are just the enemy strongholds, and they need to be brought under control if we want to stand any chance of winning this fight," Hector replied, turning to look at them. "But this means there are others. Not just other survivors, but people in power. Civilization has ended."

The excitement that peppered his voice was clear, and also chilling.

"If they are willing to mass murder an entire city, then what makes you think we would want them in charge, even if what you are saying is true?" Vanessa was in the mood for a fight and would not let Hector talk his way out of it.

"That is the way the world has always worked. Collateral Damage is what they call it. We are just lucky to have survived so far into life without ever having to be brought to face the true realities. This is the world, and this shows us there are still people out there making decisions, leading things, leading us." Hector pressed on.

"I didn't care for the crazies who chose war over peace before the dead rose, and my view has not changed since. Sacrificing innocent lives is never the answer." Vanessa stood firm.

"Well, what about killing the zeds?" Hector asked, his words were a lure, drawing the conversation down a road only he knew.

They had all learned early on that it was hard to argue with a lawyer. When Hector was in one of his moods, then he would always twist things so that people agreed with him in the end.

"That is a different story. Disassociation is not the same as sacrificing for the perceived greater good," Vanessa snapped, pleased with her response.

"Good," Taron jumped into the conversation. "Maybe we can agree on something there because those fires won't kill them all, zeds or survivors, and they will be leaving the city by the herd."

"I hadn't thought about that," Henry spoke up.

"About what?" Vanessa asked, looking at her husband.

"Think about what happened yesterday. That was just from a fire in the power station outside of the city. Now the entire city is burning to the ground. Those things are going to be coming out by the thousands." The words hung heavy in the air, and for the next few moments, nobody spoke.

"We need to leave," Taron said.

"Nonsense," Hector replied quickly. "We stay underground. They are mindless, they will walk right over us."

"Can you guarantee that?" Taron asked.

"Have you ever seen one stop and try a door? What are the chances they break into the shelter, look under the beds and find our basement entrance, open it up and come down to fucking eat us?" Hector snapped, his temper fraying.

"I don't say this often, but Hector is right," Vanessa answered, her words silencing the men.

"You really think we should stay here?" Taron said, staring at Vanessa.

"Yes, Hector is right. Those things will walk us down if we try to run now. There will be too many of them, and God knows how many other cities got the same treatment." Vanessa looked at Taron as she spoke, one hand wrapped tightly around James' shoulders, holding him against her.

Henry moved forward and slid his hand around his wife.

"We have enough supplies to last us a long time. We have ammunition to fight our way out if needed. It makes the most sense," Henry said. "How long do you think we have until the first ones arrive?"

"No idea. I mean yesterday they came from closer, and now, there is more obstruction, I'd say by nightfall, certainly by sun up," Hector said, staring at the burning city.

"We can't make it that far on foot, man." Henry returned his gaze to Taron, who stood silent, lowering his head as acceptance embraced him.

"Then let's get busy. We need to secure whatever we can inside, no point in leaving things out in the open. I want us armed around the clock too. The posties may not figure out where we are, but survivors ... you bet your ass they will know where to look."

The group took one last look at the ruined city, before heading back inside, sealing their hidden entrance as best they could. Moving through the tunnels and back into the hidden bunker, none spoke.

Even James offered no resistance when he was told to stick close to his mother. There was no time to let him sit around in the shelter, however. There was much work to be done, and every hand was needed in order to salvage as much as possible before the inevitable swarm arrived.

James and Vanessa got to moving as much as they could from inside the shelter down into the second level. With conditions already cramped down there, they knew anything they opted to take down would impact their space. Everything counted, and that included the inches they left over.

Henry headed outside, hurrying to secure their garden area as best he could. Hauling as many branches and loose pieces of debris from the surrounding area, he did the best he could at blocking off the small allotment. It was not much, and they had the space for more, but the time invested in the concept of fresh produce meant it was worth trying to save.

Hector moved into the trees, looking to find any possible sources of meat. Even a handful of rabbits would give them some fresh meat and give them more time before they had to break into the canned supplies.

Taron started by clearing out the lookout hut. They had several boxes of ammunition stored there, along with several rifles, all of which would be useful to them, at some point, and they could ill afford for them to be left so open, for anybody with half a brain to spot and collect.

They moved with a fluidity drilled into them through years of preparation. Through hours of crazy plans and talks that made them the laughing point for many who knew them and of their crazy hobby.

Each of them carried a radio and would check in every fifteen minutes, to make sure nothing had happened. At the first sign of trouble, they would run to the second level shelter and wait it out.

"Mommy, are we going to die?" James asked his mother as they sorted through the fresh produce, ready to take it downstairs.

"No, no honey, we're not going to die," Vanessa answered, her words far more convincing than she expected them to be.

"I'm scared," James spoke again. Fear had stripped him of his young bravado and left him a scared little boy. A young child, he should not have known the world as they lived in it. He should have been outside playing ball with his dad, not learning to shoot a crossbow at a reanimated corpse. Vanessa stared straight ahead for a moment, letting the tears fall as they needed. She held more than enough sorrow inside her still to keep the tear jar full, but sometimes, a few needed to escape, if not just to make room for the fresh batch to be produced.

Turning around, Vanessa looked at her son, crouching down to his level before she spoke.

"We are all scared, each and every one of us. You shouldn't have to live in a world like this, but we are here, and you know something? It's all right to be scared by it. It is okay to be afraid and know what scares you. The trick … the trick is not to give up. Do you understand?" She placed a hand on James' shoulders and looked into his eyes. They were a deep green color, just like his father's, and it broke Vanessa's heart to see the pain welling behind them.

"I understand, Mommy. It's just … I miss my friends, and I miss Granny and Grandpa, too. Do they have an underground house where they live, too?"

Vanessa wiped away a fresh trail of sorrow from her eyes and paused to take a deep, shuddering breath. She could feel her heart breaking in her chest as she looked straight into the green eyes of a child who, despite everything going on, retained the youthful innocence the world seemed so determined to strip away from him.

"I don't know, honey. I'm sorry." Vanessa pulled James against her, holding him tight.

"I miss Freddie," James said, pulling away from his mother. "Is Freddie in Heaven, Mommy, or did he turn into one of the monsters?"

Vanessa broke in that moment, and there was no stopping the tears that flowed from her eyes. "I know he is in Heaven. He is playing fetch with Uncle Jonah right now." The words were a struggle to speak, and yet they seemed to give comfort to her son, so he could move from being the young child he was to someone far more mature in the blink of an eye.

"I hope so. I wouldn't want Freddie to be running around biting people." James lowered his head and stared at the ground, giving Vanessa the chance she needed to wipe her eyes and force the mask of composure back into place.

"Come on, we had better get back to work. We have lots to do," she said, placing a hand on James' shoulder.

"Ok, Mommy." James nodded, looking up again, his eyes were bright and he smiled, taking the linens his mother handed him, without complaint.

***

Beyond the compound, everything felt too still. After the rumble of the jets gave everybody a moment of buoyancy, a concept that everything was going to be all right, they found themselves adrift. Only now, the sea was more turbulent than ever, and the life raft they were crammed into was leaking air faster than any of them could blow it in.

Hector stood in the trees, his back to camp, and sank to the floor. Even though he was only a few hundred meters away, it felt as if he were at the end of the world, and the rest of the population were all running the other way.

Sitting on the floor, he watched as a spider nimbly made its way down the side of the tree opposite him and disappeared into the sparse foliage. Hector had always feared spiders. He laughed at the concept now, however. He laughed at all his fears. In light of the utter terror that was the real world, shallow rooted fears and phobias seemed crazy to him.

In the distance, something snapped, a twig or a branch. Snatching up his rifle, and with the sheath of his knife unclipped, Hector shot to his feet and moved off toward the source. His footsteps were soft as he made his way deeper into the woods.

He knew better than to stray too far from camp, but the idea of fresh meat was a compelling one, and he knew time was of the essence. The city would be emptying more and more with each step he took, which meant the droves could be heading their way in numbers too great to count.

Another snap to his right brought Hector to a sudden stop. Had the target changed direction, or was it not prey he was chasing, but rather running into the hungry arms of the next generation of predators.

Lowering his rifle, and swapping it for his knife, Hector ducked behind a tree and composed himself. He couldn't see the camp anymore but knew exactly where he was.

Peering from behind the tree, he saw the shambling dead figure walking toward him. The man was wearing a torn tank top and a pair of running shorts. His wiry frame and frizzy hair made him look quite the picture. His body was covered in lacerations, and from the bulge around his shoulder, something had been broken or popped out of place.

The zed had not seen Hector yet, for it continued to amble its way in a straight line, heading right for the camp.

Hector tightened his grip on the knife and tried to calm his thundering heart. Sweat ran from his brow and burned in his eyes. When with the group, he was able to mount the cold-hearted façade, because out of all of them, that is who he was, but alone it was a different story. There was no backup, no band of brothers looking out for each other.

Steadying himself, he listened and counted. The slow gait would mean slower steps and more of them. The growls grew louder in his ears. Twigs snapped as the gangly zed's shadow appeared on the ground.

Two more steps, then we do this.

The stench of its rotting flesh traveled ahead of it, like a warning shot fired into the masses. The taste of it was still enough to make Hector's stomach churn.

One ...

Hector raised his knife, ready to kill. Not that it would make a bit of difference, killing one of them, but the minute they stopped to think about the futility of fighting back, was the minute they signed their own death warrants.

Come on you bastard ... two.

Hector spun around the tree, his arm rising as he did, so that as he moved square on to the dead man, his knife was already descending. Coming down from a high angle, the blade slid into the side of the dead man's head, entering just above the ear, and sliding through until the hilt, even with minimal thrusting pressure applied.

The tip of the blade broke the skin on the lower right-hand side, and with wide eyes, the thing slid to the floor. Hector was sure they did not even know that death was coming for them. They had a hunger that ate at them like a sickness. It consumed them until there was nothing left.

It was not just the zeds that did not see things coming. Hector too was caught off guard when the second set of hands fell on him. Rolling on instinct, he ended on his back, pinned beneath a female zed, whose snapping and snarling teeth were but centimeters away from Hector's neck.

The dead weight of the woman, who in life could not have weighed more than a hundred and fifty pounds, crushed him, taking both his arms just to keep her from sinking on top of him.

Hector gritted his teeth and heaved, aware that his hands were gripping the woman by the breasts. Her saggy tits were not only the most logical thing to grab given their size but also meant his fingers could sink into the dead flesh and grant him some extra purchase.

Hector struggled and tried to bring his legs up and beneath the woman, looking for some extra leverage to buy him some time. A thick strand of putrescence fell from her mouth like drool. It was cold and slimy as it ran down the side of Hector's neck.

With a sudden jerk of his body, Hector managed to bring his knee upwards and into the woman's flank. He drove his leg up once, twice, and then a third time. Each time he heard the satisfying snap of bone as ribs broke from his assault.

It was only after the third strike that the dead woman's weight shifted enough for her to be thrown free. Tossing her to one side, tearing her shirt free in the process, Hector rolled to his feet, gasping for breath, and dizzy from the exertion. His knife was on the floor, too far to grab without another strike. He strode toward the woman and punted her head with the toe of his work boot. Catching her square on the jaw, he kicked the lower left-hand side of her face free, leaving it hanging on by the right-hand jaw joint. Black blood spurted up into the air like a rotten fountain, and the smell that rode with it was overpowering.

The woman seemed not to notice that her face was missing such a vital component, and continued to thrash on the ground, reaching for Hector, hungry desire filling her eyes.

Bending down, Hector collected his knife and stared at the woman.

She could not have been that long into her twenties, and from the look of her body, she had taken care of herself. Dropping to his knees, he trapped one arm beneath him and stabbed down through the center of her forehead. She fell still instantly. Hector pulled his blade free and was instantly hit by a case of the shakes.

He couldn't catch his breath, and the world began to spin. Darkness threatened to claim him, but Hector forced himself to stand. Leaning against the nearest tree, he held himself upright and forced long deep breaths into his lungs.

After a few minutes, the nausea and dizziness passed. He began to get a sense of where he was, and his strength returned. Although a weakness had set into his legs, which he was sure would take some time to disappear.

It was the closest he had come to death since it all started, and it reinforced in his mind the knowledge of one thing. He would not go out like that. He would sooner put a bullet in his brain than risk turning into one of them.

He didn't have time to rest, however, as the sound of movement just to his left brought the fear surging through his veins. The sudden rush cleared his head.

No, it's too soon. We're not ready, Hector thought as he looked through the trees.

His head told him to expect a sea of the undead, their jaws salivating at the prospect of the five-course meal that lay ahead of them.

He braced himself, peering into the trees. He focused, prepared for the worst. Moving forward, his legs still uncertain beneath him, Hector stared into the trees.

He jumped when the body appeared, moving slowly through the trees, but he stifled the gasp before it could escape his throat, and warn the deer of his presence.

Picking up his rifle, Hector took aim and fired. His shot was not as accurate as he wanted it to be, his shaking body sending the bullet into the creature's neck rather than its head.

The deer ran a few steps, blood leaking from the hole just above its shoulder. Collapsing a moment later, it lay on the ground, crying out and kicking with its legs.

"Shit," Hector growled aloud, knowing the sound of the creature's death would attract anything within earshot.

Hurrying to where it lay, he pulled his knife and after wiping off the zed blood as best he could, he sliced the creature's neck, accidentally saturating himself in arterial spray.

Coughing as his mouth filled with blood, Hector fell to the floor once again, landing on his ass.

"Fucking shit," he growled, spitting deer blood onto the woodland floor.

The creature fell silent, and with a final kick of its hind legs, it died. Larger than Hector expected, it was going to be quite the task moving it back to the camp. He had to try, however, as leaving it even for a moment would mean losing it.

Taking hold of the creature by the legs, Hector heaved, slowly dragging the carcass back toward the camp. As soon as he came into view, he saw Taron jogging toward him.

"What the fuck happened to you?" Taron asked, the initial smile on his face sliding away when he saw the look in Hector's eyes.

"Close call with a couple of posties. Nothing serious," Hector lied, putting on the cold-hearted front.

"All right," Taron answered, letting Hector know he knew that the lawyer was lying, but was happy not to push the matter any further. "Need a hand?"

"Sure, let's get her up, been dragging her through the shit for a few hundred meters already."

Together the two men hoisted the deer into the air and carried the blood-dripping carcass into the camp.

"You do know that the blood is just going to draw them to us, right?" Taron said as they placed the deer down in what served as their front yard. Henry came walking up to them, wiping his hands on a rag.

He whistled as he got close. "Nice shot."

"Thanks," Hector answered, before turning his attention to Taron. "I've got a plan for the innards."

Hector smiled, before explaining his ideas.

Not long later, with the deer emptied, skinned, and left in Vanessa's capable hands, the three men headed off in different directions, each carrying with them a bucket of offal and a section of wet deer hide.

Hector's plan was simple, and each man nodded as he explained it.

Henry made his way through the trees to the immediate west of the camp, careful not to spill his goods until they reached the right spot. He found the old path Hector had indicated and began to walk it, letting the contents of his bucket spill to the floor ever few meters. The splash of organs, blood, and general deer juices hit the ground with a sickening splat.

Once the bucket was empty, Henry looked back at the trail he had left. He could already see flies and other insects crawling out to play. Launching the dirty bucket into the trees, he looked around for anything that would let him finish the final step in Hector's plan.

He saw a tree stump, old and long since rotted away to little more than shaped sawdust. It was perfect.

Draping the wet hide over the stump, spreading it out as much as he could, using the natural tackiness of the bloody skin to stick it in place, he stepped back. It did not look like anything to him, but to the hungry eyes of the dead, it should be enough to at least draw them in.

Hurrying back to the camp, Henry arrived just moments after Hector and a similar period of time ahead of Taron.

"Done?" Hector asked.

"Done," each man answered in turn.

"Now we wait. That should be smelling real good to those things and will get a nice group of them hanging out over here. Like you said, those things won't find us, most likely won't even know people are living here. So the more of 'em we can pull to us, the less likely any survivor types are going to come along and take what's ours," Hector said, briefly outlining his plan once more.

It was simple, use one enemy to hold off another. No group of survivors would want to attack a herd of zeds, not anybody in their right mind at least. So it would buy them time, and that was the best commodity of them all in the new world. Time to think, time to rest, and time to come up with a better plan.

The group finished up their preparations and hurried inside. Henry took one last look around the place they had built. He thought about the nights and months that had gone into building the shelter and digging the foundations for the underground level that was now going to save their lives. He thought of the plans they had and the scenarios they ran through. War, diseases, natural disasters. Only once had the rising of the dead come up, and that was just James, joking around, waving a comic he had somehow gotten his hands onto, in the air.

Henry took a deep breath, shocked at the emotion he felt, the connection he had already built with the place. He closed and locked the door, turning to face his extended family.

"Right, let's get comfortable."

CHAPTER SEVEN

Jerry woke with a jolt. The sun was streaming through the windows, and he was as naked as the day he was born. Looking around the room, he felt lost and confused.

Was it just a dream? He didn't recognize the room, but that didn't necessarily mean anything bad.

He sat up and saw his bloody clothes lying on the ground beside the bed, and everything came flooding back to him. The rising of the dead, the devastation they had seen and caused as they made their way to the city.

He remembered the car trouble, and the houses, he remembered Maddie. Suddenly the scent of her presence was on him. His head ached as he tried to make sense of what had happened. He stumbled around the room, gathering his clothes, feeling more disoriented for having a good night's sleep in a comfy bed than he had from every night spent camping in a truck surrounded by the undead.

Getting dressed, he cringed a little as the blood stains cracked and rust-colored flakes fell to the floor like bloody snow.

"Rise and shine, sleeping … oh crap, you're awake," Lou said, faking disappointment. "We got coffee brewing downstairs. Turns out whomever lived here was a coupon freak or something. You gotta check out the storeroom."

Lou left again, breezing out of the room like a man who had had too much coffee.

"Never figured you for a morning person, Lieutenant," Jerry said as he stumbled into the kitchen. Even after a good night's sleep, it took him some time to get his humor going.

"Nonsense. I've been up hours, it's practically afternoon for me. Besides, who knows when we will get to wake up in a real bed, and start cooking bacon for breakfast," Lou said, as chipper as a man who had woken up to find some young blonde's mouth over his cock.

"Did someone say bacon?" Maddie asked, her voice traveling ahead of her.

She walked into the kitchen and looked at Jerry, said nothing, and turned her attention to the stove, where a pan was sizzling, distributing a number of delicious aromas through the spacious kitchen. The combination of smells was so good that it made their stomachs hurt just to be close by.

"Well, it's bacon adjacent. Some long-life shit. They've got powdered eggs too. It won't be gourmet cuisine, but a damn sight better than what they serve back at the base," Lou said as he ran the spatula around the pan. "Grab a plate, the first round is ready. Figure we had better load up our bellies as well as the truck. Abuse good fortune when she strikes."

As the five sat around the breakfast table, they looked like the strangest family alive. They ate with an insatiable fervor, cooking pan after pan of food, shoveling it into their mouths, along with can after can of bread rolls and croissants. They devoured almost everything in the kitchen cupboards and almost fainted when Benny found a can of coffee and an old-school mocha machine.

A few moments later, they had a small, controlled fire burning in the kitchen sink, and positioned the coffee pot above it.

The air was pregnant with expectation, and Benny earmarked as being the hero of the day if everything went according to plan.

"Oh shit, Lou," Jerry said, as he looked up from the coffee pot and saw the three zeds that had wandered into the side garden of the house.

"I've got it," Maddie said, grabbing her knife from the kitchen table.

Jerry fought the urge to go after her, to help her …

To protect her?

But he held himself back, knowing the team would look at him and start pushing the issue. They had slept together, and it made no sense to him. It had been awkward, it had been aggressive, and driven by rage more than anything else. There were still too many questions to be answered, so he turned back and watched as Maddie sped around the house to meet the zeds head on.

The altercation was over in a minute, and the result was never in any doubt. Maddie's blade split the skulls of the three zeds as if they were the same warm rolls the others were slicing inside the house.

Maddie turned and made her way back to the house before the third body hit the floor. Wiping her blade on the leg of her pants, she walked back in and grabbed a bacon roll from the plate and took a bite.

"I could get used to it here," she spoke with a full mouth.

"Yeah, shame we have orders to follow," Lou answered; his words sounded harsh, but everybody could hear the regret in his tone.

"When do we head out?" Sanjay asked as he poured a cup of strong black coffee, taking his allocated ration, before filling the pot and setting it back on the fire.

"ASAP. We should load up on as much as we can from downstairs, get some wheels under us and head on up to the city," Lou replied, as he took another roll and sat down at the head of the table.

Nobody spoke for a few minutes, allowing the peace of their situation to settle. There was no telling when the next chance to relax would come along.

The kitchen was a neat and tidy affair and had clearly been the focal point of the house. State of the art machines lined the counters on the far side of the kitchen, which seemed very much split between working space and storage.

A mellow color combination of pastel yellow on the walls with a running green motif, of a similar easygoing shade, running through all the ancillary decorations, gave the room a strange Easter-like feel.

"Has anybody made contact on the radio?" Jerry asked, finally bringing the subject matter back to their given task.

"No," Maddie answered, looking up and across the table at Jerry. "I was trying this morning but got nothing but static."

"I had the same yesterday, both during the day and at night," Benny answered. "It's like the whole base just doesn't exist anymore. I mean, even if they were all wiped out, there should have at least been an open comms channel."

"It doesn't matter. Not right now," Lou answered, his voice begrudgingly leaving behind the sudden bout of suburban bliss, and dragging itself, and them, back into a world of orders, and blind faith in the chain of command. "We have a job to do, and we will do it. We have our orders. We'll cross whatever bridge we come to when we get to it, and not before."

Around the table, everybody nodded. Lou was a level-headed leader, especially in the light of the new world. Yet he made it clear then, that he was still in charge, and his lead would be followed.

"We don't need anybody looking up ahead with binoculars, spying trouble we don't know we will reach, at the expense of missing the fucking problems around us in the here and now." The air around the table changed. The transformation was complete. It was back to work. Business as usual.

"Maddie, Jerry, head downstairs and pick up as many supplies as you can get. Benny, fix that fucking truck or find us something else that moves. Sanjay and I will sweep ahead, clear out the path as best we can. Meet back here in fifteen."

The group scattered, each given their own task.

Jerry followed Maddie down to the basement, where he stood in shock at the sight of the supplies.

Large, industrial quality shelving units had been constructed along all four corners of the underground space. A quick glance was enough to confirm that everything was sorted in the same way you would expect to find them in most supermarkets.

Jerry ran his eyes over everything, affording himself a few moments to take everything in. His mother had always had a cupboard stocked with supplies, but nothing compared to the size and spectacle that stood before him.

Not only were there washing detergents and fabric softeners, in all different scents and flavors, but sizes too. Sorted from the bulky budget buy boxes on the bottom shelf, up to the half-liter refill packs on the top.

Cosmetics and bathroom products, canned goods in the form of soups, vegetables, meatballs, cocktail sausages and more filled the room, each one lined up perfectly, turned to ensure the labels were all square on to the room. There was an entire shelf dedicated to razor blades, and two to shaving creams and foams. Sponges, both of the kitchen and bathroom variety painted a rainbow of colors over one shelf, while bleaches, oven cleaners, and multi-purpose sprays offered a safe haven to almost all levels of germaphobes known to man.

"Bingo," Maddie spoke up to his far left.

She had wandered off into the basement and pulled back a blanket to reveal a supply of water that could have sustained their entire regiment, let alone just the five of them.

"Let's start hauling this shit upstairs." She didn't look at Jerry as she spoke, even turning the other way as she picked up the first load of water and started walking back.

Jerry followed her, unsure of how to handle their new situation. Was she ignoring him because she was ashamed? Maybe because she felt guilty for it, or God, perhaps it was simply because she didn't enjoy it? The thoughts bounced around Jerry's head like a ricocheting bullet in a cartoon.

Carrying a load up the stairs, they passed one another, Maddie squeezing herself against the wall to let Jerry past. For a second, Jerry thought about pausing and asking Maddie what was going on, but he knew better than to try it. Instead, he just looked at her. She was beautiful, and even a quick glance was enough to remind him of that fact. Their eyes met briefly, and Jerry saw something flash in them. Not regret, not shame, but something else. Something that Maddie was struggling to keep under control. Her amber eyes seemed to glow as if on fire, as if the inferno raging beneath the surface had flared up, threatening to consume her whole.

Load by load, they brought up the water, pausing to drink a bottle each, enjoying the cool, but not cold, liquid. It was hot in the cellar, and the more stuff they moved, the warmer it became. Both were sweating profusely by the time they were done, and their scent filled the small space like an old-school gym at the end of a summer day.

"About last night," Maddie said, speaking up as she passed to take another drink of water.

"We don't need to," Jerry lied.

"Yeah, we do. It was good, I had fun, but I am not looking for some relationship, or anything. I was stressed, couldn't sleep, and you were there." Her words were cold, but there was something behind them, something warmer.

"Makes sense," Jerry said, once again confused as to what he should be feeling.

"In fact, yours wasn't even the first room I went into. You were just the only one still awake," Maddie lied, adding venom to the words as a way to distance herself from any personal attachments. Her default setting was to take and then discard.

"Oh well, I get it. These are crazy times," Jerry said, knowing he should feel hurt by what she had said. At the very least his male pride should be bruised, but all he felt was a need to move closer.

Maddie didn't react to his coming closer, in fact, she seemed to shuffle closer to him in response.

"I mean it. It meant nothing," she said, their bodies so close the warmth radiating from one was felt by the other.

"I believe you." Jerry paused, and moved forward, his intentions clear, when suddenly, noises from up in the house shattered the moment that was starting to happen. Their quest for something private, in a world that had stripped them of everything; even down to the last shreds of human dignity, would have to wait.

Maddie collected an armful of canned veggies and soups, while Jerry grabbed several armfuls of long-life milk, instant coffee granules, and sugar. He paused briefly to force a couple of boxes of protein bars into the pockets of his trousers.

He reached the kitchen to find nobody there. The silence confused him for a moment, but when he saw the table was empty of their supplies, he reasoned they had gotten the cars fueled and ready and were loading things up.

His mind was still partly distracted by the lingering memory of Maddie, but soon cleared when the first gunshot rang out. Dropping his supplies to the floor, Jerry burst forward, unarmed but ready to rip the undead apart with his bare hands if needed.

He came to a sudden halt when he saw the rest of his group on their knees, hands on their heads. Sanjay's near headless corpse lay on the floor, twitching as the final seconds of his life bled from what remained of his skull.

Behind the body, stood a man with a shotgun. His tattooed arms clutched the weapon across his bloated belly. He stared at the corpse with a cold fascination, before turning his attention to the others.

"It doesn't have to be this way," he spat. "You play ball, and you get to live."

"You're making a mistake," Lou growled at him. "We're military, you shoot us, we all come after your ass."

The fat man chuckled. "Aw shucks, cap'n. We're all ex-military here. The world is changing. I did my duty out there and got fucked in the ass when I got home. You think because you serve that you get a pass. Fuck no, son."

The reference to the military seemed to agitate the man, but it gave Jerry a moment to back away from the doorway. He had been caught unawares and stranded in a position which, had the man moved a pace to his left, would have left Jerry a sitting duck.

As it was, he hurried backward, disappearing around the corner of the hallway. From there, he turned around and hurried upstairs. Grabbing the rifle from his bedroom, he checked the clip, took off the safety and prayed he wasn't going to be too late.

The master bedroom gave the best view of the front of the property, and the two groups that occupied the garden.

Two four-by-fours and an old, beat up panel van were parked along the roadside. Jerry could see two men inside each of the vehicles, while the panel van was open, with two men loading their supplies into the back. One had long blond hair, which looked like a mullet, while the other was an older man who moved with a pronounced limp. By the house, he counted the fat man, and another fellow who, judging by his build and initial appearance, could well have been a brother. There was at least one more man there, although the house just blocked him from view.

Training or not, they were at the disadvantage, and any action he took, would have consequences.

"Thank you very much for bringing the supplies out to us. We appreciate all your hard work," the voice of the hidden member of the group said. "As thanks, we might just leave the rest of you alive."

There was a laugh; a crazy, deranged sounding laugh, which spread through the two other men standing close by.

"Then again," the voice continued, "maybe one more is needed, just to get the message across. You know, that you don't fuck with the New Outlaws."

The laugh came again, and as some signal was given, the fat man raised his rifle and positioned himself behind Maddie.

Time slowed down to a crawl. Jerry felt his world change, an experience he had only had once before, and that was out in Iraq when an IED took out the lead car in their convoy.

It was as if his senses were heightened by some superpower or another. He saw things in such detail. The look of understanding that hit Maddie's face, when she heard the crisp click of the shotgun being readied to fire. He saw the look of near delight spread across the fat man's face.

It all happened in the blink of an eye. Jerry didn't have time to think, he just took aim and pulled the trigger. Time seemed to freeze, and then suddenly a hole appeared in the would be executioner's face, blooming like a black hole in the space where his nose had been. The bullet bounced around inside his head, scrambling what few brains he had, before exiting the rear side of his head. Blood misted the air, while chunks of bone and brain matter rained down on the ground.

The body hit the floor, and just before everything sped back up again, Jerry saw the hidden figure emerge. He held a pistol aimed at the group. Squeezing off another shot, Jerry winged the man on his shoulder, causing him to drop the gun. Fire was returned by the second fat man and the group from inside the cars.

Jerry ducked down, moved to the next window, and fired a sustained burst at the cars, not hitting anybody, but doing enough to scatter the group, including the young woman who had been with them. He could make out that her hands were tied and her face looked a bruised mess. He wanted to yell at her to run, to try to escape, but there was no time. Looking back at his group, he saw them jump to their knees and charge down their captors. Maddie took out the second fat man, throwing a swift jab into his throat, before an elbow split open his eyebrow, painting his face a dark crimson. A shot to his nuts brought the man to his knees. Another gunshot cracked out. Maddie turned, giving her foe the chance he needed to half run, half stumble, out of the way, his top-heavy physique barreling him forward while preventing him from achieving a full vertical base.

Maddie disappeared from view, along with Lou and Benny. Cursing, but sure the three of them could handle themselves, Jerry retrained his rifle on the cars. The young girl had indeed tried to run but was being hauled back to the car by her hair. Checking his sights, Jerry did not have the angle to make the shot as they disappeared behind the panel van.

All three vehicles started up, and while a burst from his rifle peppered the panel siding with holes, he did little to halt their escape.

The cars sped away, the panel van side door opening further down the street, to allow a shorter, bulky-looking man the chance to leap in.

Jerry reasoned he was the owner of the unidentified voice, which meant one man remained from his initial count, not including the fat fuck who was bleeding out all over the lawn.

Hurrying back downstairs, Jerry found himself unusually worried about Maddie. He knew he shouldn't have been so afraid, for Maddie was probably tougher than all of them. As he got downstairs, the group was manhandling the young man unfortunate enough to be left behind.

Unlike the rest of his crew, he was a gangly, weak man who lacked the intestinal fortitude to play the role of villain, even in the new world. This was further evidenced by the stream of vomit that covered the front of his shirt. His stomach unable to accept the facts he had witnessed, and the combined knowledge of the role he played in it.

"Listen, son," Lou began, as Benny and Maddie stood beside their captive, holding him in place. "Your buddy out there is bleeding all over the place, and the rest left you. They abandoned you. That's how little you mean to them. You don't leave a team member behind."

On the chair, the man, who Jerry, on closer inspection noticed was really not much more than a kid, squirmed and tried not to cry.

"You can't kill me. The New Outlaws will be back, and they will have an army with them." His words were tough, but the break and squeak in his voice told more about his fear than his bravado.

"Well, you got balls, kid. Shame you're never going to get to use them." Lou lowered his hand to his gun, and the kid screamed, pissing himself at the same time.

"Oh, Jesus Christ, would you look at that. He made a mess on the fucking floor. Ugh." Lou sighed in an over-exaggerated motion. "What's your name, son?"

"Lucas," the kid replied, sniveling.

"Well, I'll tell you what, Lucas." Lou crouched down as he spoke. "You tell me where your buddies are, and I'll let you live long enough to get your dick wet with something other than the grease of your own palm. What do you say?"

"I can't give them up. They saved my life," Luas answered, coughing and sniffing.

"That may be, but they also sacrificed it at the first sign of trouble. So what's it going to be? Will you help us, or do I turn your face inside out and leave you for the bugs?" The anger in Lou's voice had Jerry believing that their lieutenant actually would pull the trigger.

"I can't," Lucas wept.

"It's all right, Lucas, you tell us where they went, and we will take care of the rest. You can disappear in the other direction, and nobody will be any the wiser." Lou's tone changed now that he had Lucas on the ropes.

"They … they have a place, like a farm or something, a few miles from here. It's off the highway, down some dirt road. They never shared the address with me, and I'm not from around here." Lucas' voice steadied. Whether it was because he believed that Lou would ensure his safety, or because he had accepted death as the ultimate inevitable, he couldn't say.

"Thank you, Lucas, you made the right choice here." Lou rose from the squat he had fallen into and clapped a hand on the kid's shoulder.

"You can have the house if you want, we were done with it anyway. Hit the road when you are ready and don't look back," Lou said as both Benny and Maddie walked away.

As expected, Lucas didn't move. He remained sitting the entire time, weeping and muttering to himself as they loaded up their van with the rest of the supplies from the basement store. Even as they drove away, they saw his shadow still sitting in the same chair, as if they had forgotten to untie him.

With the four of them, their weapons, and all the supplies, the luxury edition minivan seemed a lot smaller than it was. They pulled away from the house, driving out of the warren of suburban life, and onto the main road into the city. In that time, nobody spoke. It was only when Benny pulled the vehicle over to the side and slammed his arm into the side of the door, releasing a pent-up roar of animalistic brutality that the silence was broken.

"What are we going to do, LT?" Maddie asked, looking at Lou.

Lou turned in his seat and looked at what remained of his team. "Any luck getting the base on the radio?" he asked, looking at Benny, acting as if he nothing was wrong.

"No, there's no answer. The channel is open, but if anybody can hear us, they're not answering." Benny calmed his rage, and his words sounded, all things considered, to be calm and serene.

"We have a job to do. We were sent here to scout out survivors, check out the cities." Lou paused for a moment, focusing himself. "The way I see it, we found some survivors already. It's only fair that we go pay them a visit."

It took a second for the words to sink through the fog-like haze that had wrapped itself around the group.

"Fuck yeah," Benny spoke, as soon as the penny dropped.

"Just drop in and see how they are coping, it's the right thing to do," Maddie offered, her eyes glinting with the wind of the devil behind them. She turned her head and looked at Jerry, smiling.

"I agree, I mean there could be all kinds of crazy folk out there. We need to make sure they are safe." Jerry grinned.

"That settles it then," Lou spoke. "We have new orders. Benny, you remember those directions?"

"Like they were tattooed on my eyelids, Lieutenant," Benny answered.

"Great, then we head that way. But we are not rushing in all gung-ho. We do this properly. We recon first, check them out, see what they are doing. Who knows how many they have at this compound. We are doing this for Sanjay, but that doesn't mean we lose our heads." Lou stared at each of them in turn.

He knew all too well how the red mist could descend and dislodge all concepts of reason and consequence. They had to be smart, because Lou understood, that even though those asshats were crazy, they had been right about one very simple thing. "The world isn't how it used to be. We don't know what lies down the road, or around the next bend. We are a team, and we will function that way until the end. Got it?"

"Yes, sir," the three of them answered in unison.

They pulled away from the curb and drove back through the empty suburban homes. The dead were scattered around the gardens, wandering aimlessly, but they had lost interest in taking potshots from the passenger seat.

Maddie watched the houses go by, her mind a whirling storm of thoughts and emotions. She saw the dead inside their homes, staring out of the window, as if some part of their brains still remembered, or longed for better days. For a moment, she felt sad for them. The dead didn't ask for this. Nobody did. But that did not change the fact that they were killers and needed to be stopped.

Beside her, Jerry sat staring out of his window. His eyes scanned the wandering zeds, still unable to get his head around the beginning of it all. Nobody seemed to know where it started, or what had caused it. They simply went to bed one night and when the morning broke, so rose the dead.

He stared in cold fascination as they drove past an expansive garden, where a ride-on lawn mower stood abandoned. Protruding from beneath it, was a dead man, his legs hidden by the machine, but the splatter of blood and meat over the neatly maintained lawn told Jerry all he needed to know.

How many people were gone? He had no idea, but judging by what they had seen so far, there were not that many folks left around. He hoped he was wrong. They had not been inside many real metropolitan areas. He hoped, beyond all reason, that people had found a way to escape the new world.

People like Mark Cavanaugh, his oldest friend, pre-dating his military career by almost a full decade. Mark was a good, decent, hardworking guy, who had no luck with women. When he finally found Mrs. Right, he married her within months, and quickly expanded his family with two children. Then tragedy struck, and his wife, Denise, died suddenly in her sleep. She wasn't sick, she didn't smoke, but her body just gave up one night.

The idea of Mark being dead didn't sit with Jerry.

What about his kids? he thought, before answering himself just as quickly.

Shut up. Don't start thinking like that.

Shaking his head, Jerry was glad to leave the suburbs behind. Looking over at Maddie, he smiled. Whatever was going on between them, he liked and wanted more. Not just the sex, while that had been amazing thus far, it was something deeper; a connection they shared. He wanted to explore it more, but at the same time, understood that the timing sucked, and something as complicated as a relationship needed far more consideration now than ever before.

CHAPTER EIGHT

Climbing down from the factory roof had been easy until they realized that the bottom section of the ladder had been torn away. Somebody had clearly made the attempt to stop the zeds from climbing after them. A feat that nobody had seen the dead achieve, and which everybody believed to be impossible.

"That has to be at least ten feet," Samantha said, as she peered down over Dwayne's back.

"Yeah, but I don't think it's as bad as we think," he answered, as he continued to climb down.

His feet left the ladder, and with body strength alone, he descended, moving one rung at a time.

At six feet two inches tall, by the time Dwayne reached the bottom rung and allowed his arms to extend, he only had a marginal distance still to fall before he touched the ground. Dropping down, he landed and immediately moved to check that there were no zeds lying in wait, or trapped, ready to catch anybody unsuspecting.

"It's all clear," he spoke, keeping his voice as quiet as possible, for fear of alerting anything nearby as to their presence.

Samantha followed Dwayne's lead and nimbly made her way down, the muscles sprouting from her normally slender forearms.

Dropping down to the floor, the distance a good foot further for her, she landed gracefully and silently, moving straight into a crouch. She looked up at Dwayne and smiled. "That was fun."

One by one, the others made it down. Jared and Ian came next, with Abby moving behind. Her pace was slow and robotic. She stared ahead, not looking down, moving after the others, like a machine on a pre-programmed setting.

It was as though she didn't notice the loss of support for her legs as she climbed, nor the drop that came when she ran out of ladder. Landing hard, Abby bent her knees to absorb some of the impact, but not enough to stop what must have been a jarring impact otherwise. The pain registered on her face, but it soon fell away, replaced again by the neutral, expressionless look.

Dwayne shuddered. There was something about the blankness of her stare. It made her look hollow on the inside, and more like the dead they were trying to avoid, than one of them.

Julie came down behind Abby, and the moment she touched the ground, she sought her out and pulled her close. Julie had taken charge of Abby's wellbeing, and nobody was going to hang around and argue the point.

Jared had pointed out the best choices for transport, and while the dead appeared to have been taken care of, there was no way of knowing for sure that more were not lurking close by.

"Hurry up," Dwayne called up to Ronnie and Jack who were moving down the ladder.

"Pump your brakes, dude," Ronnie said, as he climbed down the final few rungs, even hanging on one hand for a second, showing off for the group.

"Yeah, very good, you're a regular chimpanzee," Dwayne laughed, clapping Ronnie on the back once he landed on the ground.

"Just leaves you, big man," Dwayne called up to Jack.

He had also fallen silent since Kate's abduction. Nobody understood the nature of their friendships, but it was clear that the three shared a bond and deeper connection than the rest of them.

"You can do it," Julie called up to Jack, taking the place of both Abby and Kate as his cheerleader.

"Yeah, come on, buddy, you got this," Ronnie spoke up, appearing beneath the ladder, watching Jack move down. "Just take your feet off, hang a second and drop. It's not that far."

Julie turned her head to look at Ronnie, who smiled at her. "Hey, I'm not always an asshole," he said, with a wink.

Leah moved beside Ronnie, putting her arm around him. She kissed his cheek and whispered something to him. From the look on her face, Julie assumed it to have something to do with dropping his macho image and being the nice guy she knew him to be.

Julie never understood why guys needed that outer shell. Women were bitchy, sure, but at least you knew if someone didn't like you, or was a stuck-up bitch by default. Guys made it so freaking hard to tell.

Jack's feet left the ladder. He caught his body weight for a second and looked down. He stared at the ground but was more concerned with the three dead men that were approaching them all.

"Guys," he said, struggling to hold himself and speak at the same time.

"You've got it, dude. The hard part is done," Ronnie called again.

"Behind you," Jack managed to squeeze the words out before he dropped to the ground.

The impact was hard, but he crouched down to absorb as much as he could. Ronnie's hand appeared to help him back to his feet. "Nice one, bro," Ronnie said, clapping him on the back.

"Thanks," Jack answered, a little confused, but not objecting to the new niceties.

"There are zeds coming," Jack spoke, just as he heard Jared grunt.

"Yeah, our resident psycho is on the case." Ronnie pointed over his shoulder, where Jared was pulling his knife from the first post-human's skull and moving on to the second.

Dwayne moved in also, coming around from the side, swinging a lump of wood that he had ripped from a nearby pallet.

The weapon cleaved a hole in the side of the dead man's head, and while thick black pus leaked from the wound, it did not stop its advance. Another strike broke the wood and sent the creature to the floor. Dropping down, Dwayne raised the wood and struck downward. He missed the target as the dead man was far stronger than he looked and almost managed to buck Dwayne off completely. The wooden shard pierced the zed's chest, with a wet rip, much to the creature's annoyance.

Jared was on hand to catch the creature on the side of the head, shattering its jaw, before he dropped to one knee and drove his blade through the dead man's temple, ending its suffering once and for all.

"Dude, they're not fucking vampires, you don't need to stake them," Jared said, forcing a joke.

"Sorry, he moved," Dwayne answered back, getting to his feet.

"Sure thing, Buffy," Jared replied, wiping his blade on the dead man's shirt. Dwayne did the same to his hands, trying to wipe away the foul-smelling zed juices.

"Is everybody here?" Dwayne asked, looking around the gathered audience.

"All present and accounted for, Chief," Samantha answered, with a flirty smile and a devilish glint in her eyes.

"I say we take two cars, that way if anything happens to one, the others can get away, or we pile in together and make a break for it. Try to take something hardwearing, and with a full tank. I have no idea if the fuel stations are still working, and I'm keen to get as far away from things as we possibly can before we have to change up again." Dwayne had moved into the leadership role without a hitch, and as he gave the orders, he understood the pressure that was suddenly on his shoulders. Their lives were in his hands, so long as he was calling the shots.

Suddenly, the world seemed that much more aggressive. Danger lay everywhere, not just behind the snarling teeth of the post-human apocalypse, but in the heads of the other survivors. Everybody was a threat, and they could not afford to think differently. Every first contact needed to assume the worst because he would be damned if another one of their group would die because of his actions, or lack of them.

The parking lot out the front of the factory had several options, and after quick discussion they chose a Grand Cherokee and a large Chrysler; partly because of the size, but also due to the fact they both had keys, a full tank of gas and, most importantly, they were automatics, because nobody in the group knew how to drive a stick.

"Let's load up on some supplies, just a few bits, we should look to get moving as soon as we can." Dwayne gave the order, and watched as everybody reacted to it.

People returned, carrying arm-loads of canned soup and other products. Divvying up the supplies across the two cars, again, thinking about what would happen if they split up, they were loaded and ready within twenty minutes.

Dwayne took the Jeep, along with Samantha, Jared, and Ian, while Ronnie drove the Chrysler with Jack, Leah, Julie, and Abby.

"Follow me, we need to stick together as much as possible. It would be great if we could find some way to stay in touch with one another, but right now, we've got nothing, so just stay close." Dwayne spoke through his open driver's window, to Ronnie, who had swung the Chrysler around to be able to speak in the same fashion.

"Got it. What happens if we meet anybody along the way?" Ronnie asked.

Dwayne flinched. *We keep driving. Don't stop for anybody.*

"We play it by ear. There will be good people out there, but we cannot trust blindly," Dwayne said.

"Got it," Ronnie answered, giving a mock salute.

Dwayne laughed. It felt strange but good.

"You guys ready?" he asked, aware that he was stalling for time.

Nobody replied, but six eyes stared back at him, silent through fear and relief. They had survived something none of them had ever expected to be caught up in but had lost one of their own in the process.

Pulling out of the factory lot, they turned to the right and followed the road. The scattering of cars was minimal, and with some careful maneuvering they were soon on the motorway around the city, and eager to put everything behind them.

"Where are we going?" Samantha finally broke the silence.

Dwayne took a deep breath, composing himself before he answered. "I don't know."

"We should look to get out of the city, put as much open space around us as possible." Ian took the chance to speak. He and Jared sat on the back seat, and from the nervous glances Ian continued to throw his way, it was clear that he did not feel comfortable sitting beside a man he considered unstable.

"We should look to find a place to hole up," Jared spoke, looking at Ian. "Rich boy is right, somewhere out of the city, with enough land to fortify. A farmhouse or something would be perfect. We can unload our supplies, lay low and decide on our next move."

"That settles it then, we keep moving until we find a place to make camp," Dwayne said, his sentence ending early as he tried to swerve out of the way of a lumbering, bloody husk of a man who appeared from between a cluster of four crashed cars. With not much room to move, given the guardrail on the other side of the road, Dwayne managed not to hit the creature head on, but rather, caught it with the front edge of the vehicle.

The thing's body exploded in a mushy mess of black gore. The driver's side window was covered in the smeared remains of the undead balloon that had just burst against it.

Dwayne kept driving, mowing down a second group of the zeds, who disappeared under the car, and burst without giving the suspension a workout. Behind them, the second car had a much cleaner run, once the Jeep had cleared the path for them.

Suddenly the road opened for them. Two lanes became three, and not much farther, three became four. Each lane was open, with not a car to be seen. Dwayne put his foot down, letting the powerful engine stretch its legs a little.

"Got to let the beast free, every now and then." He laughed, looking across to Samantha, who sat in the passenger seat with a smile stretched across her face.

She lowered the window and let the air blast against her face.

Suddenly, the Chrysler was beside them, and both drivers were hollering as they swung from one lane to the next, enjoying the freedom.

"I think we should slow down a little," Ian said, his voice raised to combat the howl of the wind at the window.

"Oh, loosen up, Richie Rich," Jared said as he stuck his head out of the open passenger window.

"I mean it, don't you think it's strange that the cars just vanished?" Ian persisted.

There wasn't time to answer, and they were going too fast to discuss it anyway. The wall of cars appeared on the horizon and continued to draw closer to them, even after Dwayne planted his foot on the brakes.

The Jeep screeched as its wheels locked up, the rubber burning on the concrete as everybody inside braced themselves for impact.

Two lanes farther over, the Chrysler was also heading for disaster, heightened when Ronnie yanked the steering wheel and put them into a spin. The long body swung across the lanes and for a few moments, launched itself onto just two wheels, teetering on the verge of overturning, before it seemed to catch its balance and come crashing down again.

Both cars came to a stop just short of the constructed barricade, but it took several minutes before anybody found the strength to get out of either vehicle.

"Holy shit that was close," Julie finally spoke as she took off her seatbelt and opened the side panel door.

She stood up on legs that felt like jelly and immediately turned to face the other car, where her friends were all sitting, staring at the car wall before them.

"What do we do now?" she asked, her words swallowed by the wide-open space of the otherwise empty road.

The presence of the man-made wall was oddly chilling, and none of the group felt comfortable in its presence.

"Who made it?" Leah asked as she rapped her knuckles on the roof of an old olive-green sedan.

"Well, I doubt it was the dead," Jared answered, his words lacking his usual barbed edge. If anything, he was more distracted than the rest, walking up and down the structure, running his hands over it, as if he could somehow feel a way through.

A wind ran along the street, hitting the cars to create a hollow, empty-sounding cry; mother nature herself, weeping at the blockage placed in her path.

"Can we go over it?" Ronnie asked.

"Probably, but we would lose the cars and the supplies," Julie answered.

"It might be our only chance," Dwayne replied fast.

"Let's check it out," Samantha said, looking at Ronnie. "Your plan, your lead."

Both she and Ronnie made quick work of the climb. It took a moment to find a starting point, but once Dwayne took out the driver's side window of a partially crushed minivan, it gave them the step up they had been looking for.

The cars had been piled four high, with no real semblance of order. They were merely stacked in the order they arrived. It had to have been machine driven, there was no way anybody could have lifted the cars this high.

"Do you hear that?" Ronnie said as he reached the third level.

"Yeah, what is that?" Sam answered, straining to get a good ear for the noise.

"It sounds like static," Ronnie said, peering into the car he held on to. "Maybe a radio station or something."

"Could be, but it doesn't really sound like a radio." Sam's words trailed off as she made the step up to the top level of the metal wall.

No sooner had she reached it, and she turned around and vomited over the edge, narrowly missing Ronnie with her guttural expulsion.

"What is it … oh good God," Ronnie wretched, answering his own question as he reached the top of the wall.

On the other side lay a field of bodies, several deep in some places. The bloated corpses were burst open from exposure, freeing the rotting remains to flood over the road. The tarmac shimmered in the afternoon light as the sea of flies, which had been the source of the noise, jostled and bounced against one another, each bloated body eager to further indulge themselves on the presented feast.

"What happened?" Samantha asked from behind her hands.

"I have no idea, but look, there are guns and shit down there too." Ronnie pointed down to the ground, where an assortment of blood-drenched weapons

lay scattered. Some still clutched in the hands of the men and women that wielded them, while others still had a hand gripping them, but the hand itself was fully detached from the body it belonged to. Many more lay where they were dropped, as the wave of death made its march toward the city.

"Looks like they tried to set a trap for the dead," Ronnie spoke, forcing the words out quickly, to minimize how much time his mouth had to be open.

"What's going on, what do you see?" Dwayne called up, making a move to climb the wall to join them.

"Stay there, we are coming down," Samantha called down to him, her voice near panicked at the thought of anybody else joining them.

"Holy shit," Ronnie's shout made Sam spin around so fast, she slipped in the trail of her vomit and almost fell, her arms cartwheeling as she tried to keep her balance.

A gasp from below completed the moment. Ronnie reached out and grabbed Sam by the wrist and pulled her back into the middle. "Sorry," he added sheepishly.

"What did you see?" she asked, trying hard to bring her racing heart under control.

"Down there, look. They are not all dead." Ronnie pointed to the mass of bodies.

Samantha peered for a moment, taking in the ghastly scene with a near fascination. "Jesus wept," she cried out, the minute she saw the body crawling through the bloody mess.

The figure tiny, its frame torn open by bullets, the holes could be seen peppering its body like open sores. The sun and elements had decimated its body, yet still, the creature clawed its way over the dead that surrounded it. Uninterested in their rotten flesh, it had caught the scent of a far more succulent meat, and now its hunger would never end.

"What do we do?" Samantha asked, taking a step closer to Ronnie, enjoying the feeling of protection his company provided.

"We get back down and find another way." His words were calm and matter-of-fact.

Sam knew he was right, but something made it difficult for her to turn away.

"Whatever that thing down there is, it is not the person it used to be," Ronnie spoke gently, as he crouched down and swung his legs over the side of the wall.

Sam looked down at him and nodded. He was right, and she knew it, but the human condition was something that she could not just turn off. Lingering thoughts of *what if* or *maybe we could just* echoed around inside her mind. They were distracting to the point that Sam was on the ground before she realized she had even begun her descent.

Dwayne wrapped his arms around her, pulling her close. For a moment, she didn't speak. She found a solace in his arms, and in his scent, which, even after everything they had been through, still held the lingering fragrance of his deodorant and aftershave. The spice and heat made her head swim, and the feel of Dwayne's hard body pressing against her, protecting her, made Sam's head spin.

"What did you see up there?" he asked, looking down at her without breaking the embrace.

"The dead. Whoever set this up did so with fighting on their mind, but they bit off more than they could chew," Ronnie answered, as he stood in a near identical position, with Leah clinging to him, the same way Sam stood with Dwayne.

"Great, so now what?" Julie asked. She, Ian, and Jack stood a few meters back, closer to the cars, while Abby stood between them, looking more like one of the dead than ever. Her face had paled and sunken significantly in the time since they got into the cars.

"Now, we need to find another way out of Dodge," Jared said, walking toward them. Never one to stand with the group, he had been pacing the highway, looking for a new means of escape.

The highway they had been racing along was the tail end of a flyover, and as such, a short drop below them, a series of three other roads sprouted away with varying destinations advertised on the blood-smeared boards. The traffic littered highway was also scattered with zeds. They meandered mindlessly through the traffic, walking into as well as around the vehicles that stood abandoned. A few miles down the road, a larger congregation could be seen gathered around a toppled truck, which had been transporting livestock from one of the local farms. The squeals of the pigs had long since died down, but there could be no mistaking their carcasses that lay flung over the road.

As they watched, something moved among the cars. It was quick, disappearing beneath the long body of a school bus which stood with the doors open and windows broken.

"Did you guys see that?" Leah asked, pointing toward the yellow bus.

"I saw something," Dwayne answered, squinting.

"So did they." Jack pointed down to the gathering group of zeds that had all turned toward a single communal goal.

The pig appeared again, emerging from beneath the bus, crawling through the tight gap, desperate to escape and enjoy its freedom.

The moment didn't last long, as the hungry half of a broken zed caught the creature as it paused to survey its surroundings. Despite the most haunting of protestations, the pig was done for, even before the hungry jaws closed around its flank, tearing away a thick strip of raw bacon.

In a final moment of the fight, the pig, greased by blood, escaped the death hold and ran away, leaking thick sausage-like links of intestine from the fresh hole in its gut.

"We can't go down there," Sam said, staring as a group of zeds found the pig, which had collapsed, but continued to squeal, as every movement produced a fresh wave of agony.

The dead collapsed on it, obscuring the creature from view, and finally ended its pain.

"We can't stay here," Ian said.

"We could take the cars back and find another way out of the city," Julie spoke up.

"There's a lot of them down there. Could we really make it through?" Dwayne asked, watching as the dead seemed to appear out of thin air.

Suddenly, the street was filled with them. They moved in droves across the road, sweeping like a flood of decaying flesh, leaving destruction in the mindless wake.

"Is that a fire?" Leah pointed across the road, along the edge of the city, which rose to their right like the urban jungle it was.

Nobody spoke, while all eyes focused on the flames that billowed on the horizon.

"It looks like it," Dwayne said.

"That would explain why they are coming this way like that," Jared said, watching the dead with a look of near fascination. "We need to move. Get in the cars, head back to the city. Best plan we have is to settle down for the night and move on again."

When nobody raised a better idea, they split off and got back into their cars, returning the way they had come, very much with their tails tucked between their legs.

They drove in silence, watching the city loom over them. What had once been a thriving, budding metropolis had become nothing more than a prison, and the guards were ruthless and vicious.

The long shadows cast by the tall buildings and the setting sun, stretched along the roads like bars on the window of their future.

Dwayne pulled the car over to the side of the road, just short of the last exit ramp before the city proper. He left the engine in neutral and leaned forward to rest his head on the wheel. "This just cannot be happening." His words were only intended for him, and the others, realizing this, said nothing in return. They were all thinking the same thing or at least minor variations thereof. The world had gone to shit so soon. The rules of life had changed, and nobody had the chance to read the rules.

"Why did we stop?" Sam asked, placing her hand on Dwayne's shoulder.

"Because they did." He pointed back to the second car, which had stopped a hundred or so meters behind them.

Reversing up beside them, Dwayne lowered the passenger-side window and leaned forward, talking across Samantha, who sat back in the chair as if somehow needing to avoid the conversation.

"Jack says that he lives down in the suburbs here. Said his grandparents' house is there also. Big enough for all of us to hide out."

"That's the closest thing I've heard to a plan all day," Dwayne said, nodding. "You take the lead, and we'll follow, but keep your eyes peeled. Once we get off this highway, who knows what we will find."

Ronnie nodded, closed his window, and drove away. Dwayne looked through the car, his eyes stopping on each passenger in turn. None offered any resistance, and so he pulled away, watching as a long figure shambled up the road toward them.

The figure, a man, was covered in blood and walked with both a pronounced limp, and a lively gait.

Dwayne swallowed hard but said nothing. The others were too nervous to pay attention, and as they turned down the off ramp toward the road to residential paradise, the figure broke into a stumped run, his arms waving about his head.

Dwayne knew the man was human, or alive, they were all human, but he knew that the risk he posed was too great for the group, and so left him behind. He watched the man for as long as possible before he faded into the distance. Dwayne knew it was an act of murder to leave the man alone, but he had to think about the safety of the group. In a world where second chances were not given freely, every decision counted, and the tough ones needed to be made quicker and quicker.

They drove in silence, all eyes on the world beyond the car doors. The minute they pulled off the highway, the dead appeared. They moved through the streets in groups, and while the dead seemed content to let them pass through, the question of moving from the car to the house, whenever they reached it, weighed heavy on their minds.

"I hope this works," Ian said as they pulled up behind the lead car, outside a large, suburban home.

It looked like something out of a movie, far too grand to be a house belonging to an older couple, yet totally believable at the same time. An old, family home, which had stood the test of time, having witnessed the birth of all the dwellings around it; very much the king of the neighborhood.

There was no fencing or boundary wall that would act as a deterrent, other than a white picket fence, which promoted the same feeling of security as a Chihuahua as a guard dog.

They parked their cars before the adjoining garage and got out. The street was a long curving one, with this house on the apex of the turn. It afforded them a view, albeit limited, down both arms of the road. The dead milled around in groups, and there were clear signs of life in some of the other houses as evidenced by the twitching curtains.

"Are you sure we are going to be safe in here?" Julie asked as she helped Abby out of the car.

"Safer than out there," Jack replied, looking down the street, where it was impossible not to notice a few lone figures shuffling their way.

"We'd better hurry up and get inside," Dwayne spoke, having noticed the same advancements of the dead.

"They keep a spare key for the back door underneath the birdhouse," Jack said, opening the fence and letting them all through.

Abby moved under her own power, stopping by Jack to stare at him. The color was starting to return to her cheeks, and while her eyes still seemed hollow, as if part of her very being had been stripped away, she looked a lot better for it. Abby opened her mouth to speak but couldn't find the words. Instead, she leaned in and hugged Jack, her tense body relaxing as he put his arms around her in response.

"We're going to be safe here, at least until we make our next move," Jack whispered.

Abby said nothing, but Jack could feel the hot flow of tears soaking through his shirt.

The key was exactly where Jack said it would be, inside a small box screwed to the underside of the birdhouse, mounted to the trunk of a nearby tree.

"That's a step up from the fake rock trick," Ronnie smiled, clapping Jack on the back as he walked back to the group, holding the key out before him like some kind of trophy.

They opened the door and walked inside. Entering through the rear of the property, they lost site of the approaching zeds. Now, as they watched from the living room window, they saw that the creatures' attention had been taken by something else, and they had each wandered off in their own directions.

The house was as grand on the inside as it looked from the outside. The living room an open and lush affair with a real fireplace and three comfortable sofas. The kitchen was an open plan space that led into the dining room. Clean countertops and gentle paint schemes made the house feel airy and light, while wide windows caught the sun and added an additional illusion of space to the entire building.

The upstairs was equally spacious, with three bedrooms, two of which could not have been a more classic example of the 'guest bedroom', an enormous master bathroom with separate shower and bath units, and an office-style space, filled with books and a heavy wooden desk that still housed a desktop computer and a full range of stationary supplies.

"My grandfather made his money in his own business, and after he retired he decided he wanted to become a writer. He published a few books, and they were very good, but he was never in it for the money,"

Jack said as they stood in the doorway. It was the final room on the second floor of the house and officially concluded their tour. Jack had made a comment in each room, giving glimpses of his life to the group.

"If your grandparents were so rich, why did your dad work at the canning factory?" Jared asked, his words harsh, but capturing the question several of them had silently pondered.

"That's a whole other story," Jack said, not fearing the open answers he was giving. "These were my mother's parents. My birth mother. She died when I was young, and my dad, well, he was kind of an asshole. He cheated on my mom, a lot, and developed a drinking problem. They had this huge argument a year or so after my mom died. I was about six and didn't know what was happening." Jack paused, wiping his eyes.

"Yeah, my old man was a cunt too," Jared said.

"My dad was a good man." Anger brewed in Jack's voice. "He was a good man who couldn't deal with his grief. My grandparents knew this and tried to help, even after he refused it. They took care of me, and always gave me a place to come and stay. They supported Dad and helped us with a lot of things over the years. I always intercepted them, arranged it so that he never even knew it had happened. So shut your mouth, because you don't know anything."

Jared stared at Jack, before turning away from the group and storming off. Nobody spoke for a moment, but the silence was too overpowering.

"I'm hungry," Abby said, speaking for the first time since the roof of the factory.

"My gran was a great cook," Jack said, catching himself, as the emotions raged within him. "Fuck, I miss the world."

"You and me both, buddy," Ronnie said, as he put his arm around Leah and pulled her close. "You and me both."

Leaving Jared behind, the group moved back to the kitchen where they raided the expansive pantry cupboard.

Dwayne found a couple of camping stoves in the garage and a short time later, they were tucking into a feast of lukewarm canned goods, each one seasoned with a wide range of herbs and spices, in an effort to remove the tastelessness of the food.

Jared joined them, taking a can and skulking off to the living room, where he sat by the window, watching the world go dark.

An older woman in a badly fitting, brightly colored tracksuit stumbled along the fence, the sweatband that capped off her ensemble had fallen askew on her head, and as a result completely covered one eye, leaving her visually impaired. She paid no attention to the house, as she moved at a pace that probably hadn't changed much since her previously living self headed out for her fateful power walk.

The others left him be, choosing to stay in the kitchen, chatting. Jared could hear them, laughing and joking. He didn't care. Now that they had left the dorm room, the reality of life had returned. It didn't matter whether the dead were roaming the world, or if it had all been a dream and they were going to wake up and find themselves hungover and late for class. Nobody stayed around Jared for too long, and it was simpler to create the distance himself, rather than wait for them to abandon him, just as he was getting used to having them around.

Pulling his knife from its sheath, Jared studied it, looking at the faint hint of taint on the blade. He wondered if his old man had had the chance to go looking for it before the dead found him. Not that he knew if his old man would be dead, but the chance of that son of a bitch surviving was unlikely.

Jared couldn't think of anybody more deserving to be eaten alive than that prick of a man.

The knife shook before his eyes, as the tremor in his hands grew worse. Lowering the blade, Jared wiped his eyes, in case anybody came through. *Don't think like that. They will leave you anyway*, he thought to himself, wiping away the tears, nonetheless.

Returning the blade to its sheath, Jared sat back and stared. The world had gone to hell, but for the first time in his life, Jared was free. Free from the man who had dominated him for so long. From the father who didn't raise him with high fives and praise, but rather with a closed fist and a cold heart.

Jared was happy the world ended, and while it was nice to have some company, he knew that it was only a matter of time before he would be on his own again because that's the way life worked for people like him. That was what he had been taught; the lesson he had learned when his mother walked out on him, leaving him with his abuser. The lesson was further enforced when the courts ruled that his father was a fit and proper guardian for him, forcing him to live with a man who was a monster beneath the surface. A cruel and sadistic human being. Jared thought it oddly fitting that his father could be walking around out there, some mindless beast, his body torn apart and broken.

He hoped that one day he would find him, and finally end his existence. He could already feel his skin tingle at the mere thought of sliding the man's own hunting knife through his skull.

"You okay?" A voice startled Jared, who had found himself so lost in his own thoughts that he forgot his place in the real world.

Turning around he was shocked to find Abby standing in the room with him, alone and not surrounded by the new best friends she had found.

"What do you want?" Jared snapped, coming down through the haze of memories, to the reality where the screams of his demons were waiting.

"I know who you are," Abby said, her voice tiny, scared.

Jared looked at her and gave a derisive snort. "I doubt that."

"I can see through your mask. You're angry and hate the world, but underneath, you're scared." Her words hit home, and Jared felt himself flinch.

Rolling from the window, he turned to face the young woman.

"You were more fun when you weren't talking." Jared scoffed.

"You're a scared little boy, and I know why." Abby took a step closer to him.

"Really, bitch, you have no idea," Jared snarled, but to his surprise, Abby did not back down. If anything, he saw a fire in her eyes that made his skin prickle.

"I bet it was your father." She held his gaze, and Jared felt himself quiver. "How bad did he beat you?"

Jared opened his mouth, but nothing came out. His body froze, and his blood chilled inside his veins.

"Shut up!" Jared reached out and grabbed Abby by the shoulders, his knuckles turning white as he squeezed.

"Did you ever cry yourself to sleep at night, hoping he would be too drunk to come to you? Did you ever feel ashamed of hitting your period because it would piss him off so much, and just make his rage boil over?" Abby's voice rose, and she shrugged out of Jared's grip. "Did he ever fuck you so hard that your ass bled for days afterward, or beat you so bad you had to go to the hospital?"

Jared backed up a step, suddenly fearful of the woman standing before him.

"Did he ever give you a razor blade and give you the choice between sucking his cock or cutting your wrists, and then make you suck him off before he took you to the hospital to have the wounds tended to?" Tears streamed down Abby's face as she strode back over to Jared, her eyes blazed as they held onto his.

She was a wild tempest, and as Jared stood there watching her, he felt equally strong urges to both strangle her and embrace her.

"He raped me, beat me, used me in any way he saw fit. He ... he made me sleep on the floor beside his bed, chained up like a dog." Jared had never told anybody about the full extent of his abuse, not even the shrink he had been forced to go and see. Stuck up bitch that she was.

"You and I are cut from the same cloth, we're both damaged, broken even." Abby spoke with tears in her eyes but a strange defiance in her voice.

"I thought you were in love with that other girl, the one they took?" Jared said, his words still echoing on his lips when the slap came.

Abby's hand moved like lightning, and the sting it left behind caused Jared's ears to ring.

"Don't you talk about her like that. I loved her. That's the thing. When you get fucked from the age of eight, you kind of get put off at the sight of a man's cock. Kate was good and kind. She never knew the full truth, but she was all I had. Her family took me in when I ran away from home, and they made sure my old man got locked up for what he did. It was too late for me, but I played along, letting them think I was something they could fix back together again."

"I'm sorry, I didn't mean … it's just, I don't understand," Jared stuttered, caught with his mind whirling in a hundred different directions.

"You will," Abby said, moving in once more, only this time it was her lips that found Jared's face. Kissing first the hand print on the side of his face, and then his lips. "I think we can fix each other."

"How?" Jared asked, his entire body shaking.

"We go out there and take what we want, we dish out the punishment to those who need it. There are no laws in this world now, so I say we start making them before someone else does." Abby grabbed Jared's hands and squeezed, the power behind her grip surprising. "We hunt down the fuckers who are taking advantage of people like … like Kate, and we fuck them up. The others don't need to know. We can stay or we can go, either way, they are not like us."

"Where did you come from?" Jared stared into Abby's eyes, his cock hard in his trousers, and his eyes lowering to her breasts whenever he wasn't watching her speak.

"I was forged in the same place you were, and I am never going back there again." Abby was resolved.

"We will go back, one day, and we will rule the entire fucking place. Burn it down from the inside." Jared smiled, pulling Abby close to him.

He shuddered when her hand came to rest on his crotch.

"I thought …" he began, but her lips silenced him.

"Rules have changed. This is a new world, and I want to play."
Abby smirked as she dropped to her knees, while the others continued to
laugh and chatter from the kitchen.

CHAPTER NINE

The rush came, but from within the confines of their underground bunker, the true extent of it was never known. The sound of the dead battering against the outside rumbled like a strange, distant thunder. Each one of them tuned it out with relative ease.

The first two days were the hardest, the not knowing, the closeness of their new quarters, not to mention the lack of fresh air.

The first time someone took a shit, everybody realized the horrifying extent of what they had gotten themselves in for.

None of them slept well, even James sat up most of the first night, listening to the adults talk. He understood enough of what they were whispering to know they were all scared.

Even though they were only a few feet below the place they had called home ever since the world went to hell, there was something different about the bunker. It was darker, scarier. Even though they were further away from the dead, the threat they posed felt that much more intense in the dark.

On the third day, the men drew straws, and Taron was elected to head back up to the top and take a look around.

"Remember, stay low, and stay quiet. Anybody that's still out there won't be expecting you, so use it to your advantage," Henry instructed as they stood by the ladder that led back up to the shelter.

"Got it," Taron said with a smile, his words almost sounding as convincing as the expression he wore.

"No matter what, you come back down here and we make the next step together. Good or bad," Henry continued, talking to the man as if he were a child being instructed on how to behave while being let outside for the first time without supervision.

Taron climbed the ladder, moving one rung at a time. He never looked down, his attention was focused on what lay above them. The bed pushed up with relative ease, and the rest of them watched, holding their breath as he disappeared into the daylight, quickly dropping the bed back into place.

"Will Taron be all right?" James asked, holding onto his mother's hand.

"Of course he will," Vanessa lied, her mind too distracted to even try to hide the truth.

James squeezed his mother's hand tighter. It was cold, but he found comfort in it, nonetheless.

Henry saw the exchange, and walked over to them, lifting his son from the floor and into his arms.

"Taron is going to be fine. He's tougher than any of us, and he knows exactly what to do." Henry's words were comforting, and as always, James trusted them without doubt.

***

Taron held his breath as he rose up the ladder, hoping beyond everything that he would at least get out of the hatch and the bed lowered back into position before he met his end. He understood the chance of death was great, and he could accept that, but to know he was also responsible for the death of the others, especially little James, would be too much for him to take.

The bed moved back into position without making a sound. The shelter was quiet and darker than he expected.

He knew the place was empty, if not because he was still breathing, but because the air was stale. Even in the few days, they had been gone, the place had adopted the long-lost feel of an abandoned shack. Dust had settled, everything was as it had been, even the broken glass, which James had dropped as they were bringing the final things down into the bunker.

Sitting at the table, Taron let out a long sigh. It was only then he realized his hands were shaking. Taking a moment, he looked around. The darkness bothered him, playing on the few nerves he had left that were yet to be frayed by their current situation.

While nobody had actually spoken about it in the bunker, for fear of upsetting both Vanessa and little James, the thoughts had been there.

If the government still existed, and the threat was being controlled, bombing a city wouldn't stop them. Dropping a different kind of bomb just might.

"No, I'd be dead already if that had happened," Taron said, giving voice to the thoughts swirling inside his mind.

"Then why is it so dark?" he asked himself, still talking aloud.

"Only one way to find out," he told himself in a stern voice. Taron laughed, fully aware that he was starting to crack, to lose the one thing he always feared losing the most.

Moving slowly, he pulled the machete free from the sheath on his hip. The weapon was more cumbersome than any blade he was used to using, and heavy too. Hector had been insistent on him taking it, and Taron didn't want to argue with the man. Adrenaline pumped through Taron's veins as she prepared himself for whatever was waiting beyond the door. He reached for the handle and adjusted his grip on the weapon one last time. With a silent prayer on his lips, Taron opened the door and stepped outside. He knew he had promised to return with word of their situation immediately, but there were too many questions that needed to be answered. Too many risks for the others to take. He wouldn't let them die because he was too scared to take a real look around.

The day was cool, and the landscape just as dark as he expected. As if on cue, the first fat drops of rain fell. The cool water felt great on his skin, and as the heavens opened, Taron welcome it.

The zed was on him before he had a chance to realize, the hands gripping his shoulder, forcing him to the floor, as the dead man's weight pressed him down.

Taron reacted on instinct, pushing the dead man away from him, just as the hungry jaws snapped shut.

The machete had fallen to the floor and was in the dirt beside him. Not that it mattered, because there was no chance Taron could hold the creature at bay with one arm, while he turned himself enough to grab the weapon and use it.

Taron had to improvise.

Breaking the tension in his arms, and rolling with his legs, Taron managed to move the creature off balance, freeing up his right arm to go on the attack.

Balling his fist, Taron threw a punch into the man's bloodied flank. The torn and tattered flesh offered little resistance, and Taron's entire hand disappeared inside the creature. With his hands finding bone, Taron gripped the creature's spine and pulled as hard as he could, yanking until he heard the snap of breaking bone, and the pop of the zed's spinal discs rupturing.

With a final heaving effort, Taron pulled the shard of spinal column free and drove it through the side of the zed's head. Rolling away, Taron pushed himself to his feet grabbing the machete as he went.

Three came, moving from different directions. Ready for them now, Taron swung the machete and took out the first two with ease. The third had a pronounced limp, which meant the blade embedded in the creature's neck, traveling far enough to cause the head to loll to one side, but not enough to sever it completely from the body.

Four more of the dead fell upon him, converging from all sides. The hands clawed at his flesh, tearing his clothes.

Taron had expected his end to ultimately come at the hands of the dead, but he had not expected it to be so soon.

It surprised him that he did not feel more fear. It was far from a calming experience, but there was no fear. The only thing Taron felt was deep-seated blood lust. He would take as many of them with him as he could.

Raising his weapon, he drove it up under the chin of the nearest zed, watching it burst from the thing's skull in what was close to slow motion. Pulling it free, the creature fell away and another took its place. Turning, he elbowed one in the face as he pulled back his arm to strike again, the forward-moving thrust splitting a half-rotten woman's face in two along the bridge of her nose. Her eyes crossed as the bloody blade skewered whatever was left of her brain.

Taron's arm burned from swinging, while the blade felt heavier and heavier each time he hefted it. With a war cry that was created within the deepest part of his soul, Taron raised the blade again. Half a dozen zeds surrounded him. Their stench alone was enough to make his body tremble in revulsion.

Swinging the blade, he missed his target, and instead his tired strike saw the dulling blade sink into a dead woman's shoulders. Her bones snapped with a dull whisper, much like a stick filled with rot. Taron lost his grip on the weapon as the zed stumbled backward, with the blade still embedded in its shoulder.

Hands clawed at him, tearing his clothes, narrowly missing his skin. Yet there was only so far he could sink before it was over. Taron cried out but he knew nobody would hear him. He felt hands close around him, and as the world faded to black, all he could do was hope that it was not painful.

***

"He's been gone too long," Henry said, whispering to Hector.

"Then we know what it is like up there," Hector replied coldly. He showed no emotion, talking about Taron as if he had never mattered.

"You can't be serious," Vanessa said, injecting herself into the conversation, having heard every uttered word.

Hector turned to look at her. "I'm deadly serious. We go up there and whatever is there will rip us to shreds."

The atmosphere of the underground bunker grew stifling as Vanessa and Hector stared each other down. Henry stood between them, trying to negotiate.

"What about the tunnel?" he said, offering his sixth solution. Nobody said anything but both turned to look at him, which he regarded as a small breakthrough.

"What are you talking about?" Hector asked, his interest piqued, even if his mind was still made up.

"Why don't we use the tunnel, circle around through the trees and come up on the camp from the rear. We know the best routes. We can get close without being seen and take it from there."

"You really want to risk your kid for the sake of Taron?" Hector asked. "Nobody gets left behind here, it would be too risky. So either we all go, or nobody goes."

Silence fell again, as both Henry and Vanessa gave serious thought to what Hector had said. Both looked over at James, who sat on his bed reading a comic. He looked so small and innocent, yet both knew that the time of innocence was long gone.

"The world has changed. We can't protect him forever," Henry said, his resolve weak, but growing.

Henry half expected Vanessa to object, and possibly scold him for even suggesting such a thing. It caught him by surprise when she nodded.

Vanessa's gaze lifted from the floor and found her husband watching her. Her head whirred with conflicting emotions, and the overwhelming instincts of a mother's love, but she knew what had to be done. "We need to move quickly. We don't know if Taron is alive, but if he is, then his time will be running out."

"You two are crazy. Sentimentality died back when the dead rose. It was the first thing they took from us." Hector was as angry as they had ever seen him. His loud remonstrations had pulled James' attention away from his comic and over to them.

"What's wrong? Is Taron okay?" he asked, looking at each of them in turn.

Henry bent down toward his son so that they met at eye level. "We don't know. That's what we are talking about … and … well, um … you are old enough to have a say in things around here."

"Henry," Hector said again, his words soft. "Are you sure you want to do this?" It was not often that the lawyer's caring side came out, but when it did, his character changed so dramatically, it was as if he had been replaced by an entirely different person.

Henry looked from his crouch and nodded. "We were talking about going to help Taron, but it would mean we all have to go. We don't know what's up there, but if we stay here we are only putting ourselves at risk. If somebody did capture Taron, it's only a matter of time before they come for us."

James was quiet for a moment, his brow furrowed in concentration. "We need to save Taron."

The answer was resolute. The expression on the boy's face said that he knew the risks and that he had given it due consideration.

"Then we are signing our own death warrants," Hector grumbled, giving an exasperated sigh.

"We are already dead," James said, his voice was tiny, yet the words rang like gunshots.

"What?" Vanessa asked her son, shocked that such words could come from his mouth.

"We are already dead. People die every day. Now there are monsters out there that want to eat us. People still die. If we can hide here and be eaten, then why not try to rescue Taron. Maybe together we can stay alive that little bit longer."

Vanessa dropped to her knees and pulled James into a great hug.

"I love you," she whispered into his ear.

"I love you too, Mom," James replied, wrapping his arms around his mother's neck.

"You're smarter than I took you for, kid." Hector looked down at James and gave a nod. It was a strange look, and one that James did not completely understand, but he felt good for having seen it.

They wasted no time in gathering the weapons they needed. There was no need for packing anything of sentimental value, for they all realized that there were only one of two outcomes. They would survive the fight long enough to come back down and claim their possessions, or the ever-hungry dead would tear them limb from limb.

"If we are going to do this, then we need to go all the way," Hector said, as he grabbed the automatic rifles from their positions on the wall.

Handing one to Henry, Hector kept one himself, before offering a serrated-edged machete to James. The youngster took it, almost dropping the blade as the weight of his new weapon caught him by surprise.

Vanessa considered the small armory and chose a pair of Glock 17's, tucking one into the waistband of her trousers.

"We're really doing this?" Hector asked as they stood at the entrance to the tunnel.

"Yes, we are," Henry answered, letting out a heavy sigh as he did. Turning to look at his family, he smiled. "Stay close to your mother and stay safe."

James looked up at his father, and while his eyes glistened, he did not shed any tears. A small nod was the only answer he could give, and the only one Henry needed.

Opening the gate to the tunnel, they headed outside, unaware of what would be waiting for them.

***

The woods were quiet. While there were plenty of signs pointing to the passage of the city-fleeing mob, there was no immediate sign of any lingering presence.

Moving in a loop, circling back on themselves, the group headed back to their camp.

The first zed caught them by surprise, its hand snatching out from the undergrowth to grab Henry by the ankle. Stumbling, he spun around still unsure what had grabbed him. With his weapon raised, Henry was ready to fire, but all he saw were the trees.

The creature emerged from the trampled undergrowth, slithering on its belly like the serpent in the Garden of Eden. The disfigured thing, for it no longer bore any real resemblance to the human being it had once been, looked as if it had been spat from the very bowels of hell.

Reaching forward with a single arm, the other nothing but a fetid stump that oozed thick, black blood, it reached up and clawed at the ground, dragging itself closer. Its face was swollen and bloated, the skin transformed into a white, dough-like substance. While its torso suddenly deflated at around the mid-chest level. The body, beaten and broken, had burst open at the seams, under the pressure of the herd that followed it. They could make out the footprint impressions left in its softened flesh, and the bloody tracks of the feet that joined the party later.

Despite its injuries, the dead man moved on, dragging itself through the ground in search of a fresh meal. The lower half of its body was still whole, but the damage to the creature's spine, which protruded from its body at all manner of angles, rendered the lower limbs useless anyway.

Hector appeared beside Henry, and with his arm outstretched, gently lowered the firearm. "No need to draw attention," Hector whispered as he moved in front of Henry.

Striking quickly, Hector slid his knife through the zed's head and let it drop back to the dirt.

"Keep moving," Hector whispered, his voice filled with urgency.

"Dad," James called, his voice raised with shock. He pointed to the floor at Henry's feet.

The outstretched hand which had grabbed Henry's leg was still attached, along with the entire arm. Henry jumped, shaking his leg like a wild man, trying to detach the severed limb.

"Hold still," Hector said as he swung his boot at the limb, knocking it free and sending it sailing into the bushes.

"Sorry," Henry began to apologize, but there was no time. Movement in the trees told them that the fight was just beginning.

Three zeds appeared, stumbling through the trees. Their bodies were wet with rot, while the middle figure's belly was so distended it looked fit to burst without the slightest provocation.

The two men moved to engage when three quick gunshots rang out. The heads of the three zeds exploded with a damp farting noise, like old balloons.

Vanessa walked between the two men, her gun still raised and aimed at the zeds, who had fallen to the floor. She stood staring at them until the inflated man released a fart that saw his stomach fully deflate and release a gas into the air that was potent enough to kill any other creature in the nearby area.

"Oh man, that was awesome." James laughed at the fart.

"We need to move, they will be coming for us," Hector said, urging them to pick up the pace. "We need to get to the camp quickly. Anybody up there knows we're here now, so no need for subtlety."

Their pace quickened as they moved through the trees. The woodland floor had been flattened by the sheer number of those that shambled through, driven from the city by the bombs that had been dropped.

Blood and thick lumps of rotting flesh hung from branches and thorny stems, while the general stench of rot hung heavy in the air, fouling every breath they took. They didn't talk. There was no need. Their focus was clear, and as they grew closer to the camp, the sounds of a struggle came clear.

The camp yard was teeming with the dead. For some reason, they had chosen that spot to linger. A large crowd was gathered around the entrance to their shelter.

"Look," Hector finally spoke. He pointed at the crowd of zeds.

"There's too many of them," Henry whispered.

"That's Taron," Vanessa cried out, unable to control her emotions.

The two men squinted, unsure what she had seen until the foot moved. A foot on the bottom of the pile kicked out, fighting back against the weight that was crushing it.

"Move," Hector called, raising his rifle.

He let off a short burst, as he ran into the camp. Bullets peppered the flesh of the undead dog-pile, knocking the top layer away, but failing to keep them down.

A few more turned away, their attention drawn by the new guests at the party. They were met with a second burst of gunfire. The strafed shots tore through undead flesh, taking three out with neat headshots, while the final rounds tore through the throats and torsos of the approaching undead. Knocked from their feet, they floundered, trying to get up, only to be put down by Henry, who, moving in for a close-range finish, could not miss. Especially when he placed his booted foot on their chests before pulling the trigger.

While the men started to clear away the top layers of the pack, Vanessa ran and grabbed Taron's foot, pulling on his leg with everything she had. The weight was immense, and even when James put his fears aside and ran to help his mother, they made little to no progress.

"James, watch out," Vanessa called, as one of the zeds closest to them turned from the pile to chase a less crowded meal.

The thing's jaw was broken on one side, and swung uselessly from the left joint. Thick blood dribbled from the gaping wound on the right side of its face, hanging down in long strands like a dog's spit on a warm day. With a deep growl, it made a move, but James pulled the second Glock from his mother's trousers and pulled the trigger.

Firing three shots, the first went wide but somehow managed to take out the top of the skull of a smaller zed further back on the pile. The second shot tore open the zed's throat, sending gouts of the same rancid-smelling black blood spilling down the former man's chest. The third tore open his head, splitting it from the nose up.

The creature hit the floor, and as more and more of the undead turned to face the newcomers, the weight on Taron changed, and together, Vanessa and James managed to pull him free.

Unconscious and covered with blood, they managed to haul him away from the pile, which collapsed inwards on itself, as the pillar of its construction, not to mention the main focus of those caught in it, was suddenly removed.

Hector and Henry moved in, firing their guns with wild abandon. The dead were falling like flies, as blood, bone, and putrefied brain matter was spread over the ground like post-apocalyptic fertilizer.

"Watch out," Henry called as a pair of zeds came up on Vanessa from behind.

Strong, cold arms wrapped around her, grabbed her and pulled her closer. Vanessa screamed, as her body froze. She dropped the gun and felt her legs go out from beneath her.

James turned at the sound of his mom's screams, but three more shambling figures emerged. Henry and Hector moved fast, each moving down one side, trapping the dead between them. Henry fired the shot that obliterated the skull of the creature holding his wife, while Hector took care of the remaining two zeds.

There were a few stragglers left in the camp, but they were easy pickings for the two men. When all was done, there were thirty-six bodies littered around the camp, and the stench of their bloated rot hung like a smog over what had once been a haven in the midst of hell.

"Quick, let's get him inside," Hector panted. He was out of breath from the assault they had completed, and the adrenaline was already starting to ebb.

"You take Taron, I'll take Vanessa," Henry said, scooping his wife up into his arm.

Vanessa had fainted not long after she was splattered with zombie brains, but Henry caught her before she fell.

"We need to clear a path first. The bastard corpses are blocking the door." Hector kicked out at one of the bodies as he spoke. His foot disappeared into the rotten flank. "Fuck."

Hector shoved the bodies aside, throwing them with the same level of compassion one might expect from a baggage handler unloading cases from an airplane.

Both Taron and Vanessa were still out of it as the three men entered the shelter; James doing so as a man now, for after the fight they had endured, he was no longer a child in numerous ways. He didn't speak but placed the gun on the table and went to the kitchen to get a drink.

Henry carried his wife to their bed and laid her down. It felt strange knowing that they were lying above the underground bunker. Even though he had always known, something about having been down there, trapped, made it all feel that little bit different.

Taron started to stir as Hector carried him over the threshold and was soon sitting on a chair by the table. The quiet and calm, a stark comparison to the world they had just sealed themselves away from.

For a while, there was nothing but silence in the shelter. Taron sat with his head in his hands, while James, Henry, and Hector all sat with the same blank expression. Their minds busy processing everything they had seen.

Taron was the one who broke the silence when he finally started to weep.

Nobody knew what to say to offer the man any comfort. They had not found themselves buried under a pile of rotting corpses, each one intent on tearing away a mouthful of his flesh. It was James who stood from the table and put his arms around Taron, in a hug that can only be given by a child.

Henry beamed, as his body warmed from the inside. His son was good, and considering everything they had faced, he still managed to keep that spark of simple innocence. It was remarkable.

"We get to live," James said, his voice soft, not a whisper but a soft tone that carried a world of emotion that a child of his age should not need to understand or be able to add to their words.

Taron raised his head from the table. He was crusted over with gore, and a thick glob of something dangled from his ear.

"That we do … but not here. This isn't living." Taron turned his head from James and looked at the others.

"What do you mean?" Henry asked, his eyes narrowing as he looked at his friend.

"I mean this place, staying here, it's not living. We are hiding." Taron's voice gained strength as he spoke, sitting up straighter in his chair. "We built this for an emergency, to hide away and survive. That's why we spent so much money over the years. It was lunacy, but we did it, and now … now that the time has come, I realize that hiding isn't the way to live. Hiding away from the world, locking ourselves underground, we may as well be dead."

James flinched at the words, and a whimper escaped his lips.

"Taron, please," Henry said, looking at the frightened expression on his son's face. Holding out his arms, James moved to him, almost falling into his father's embrace.

"I don't mean to scare you, James, or any of you, but it's the truth. The world has changed, that's for damned sure, but the facts remain the facts. Living is about more than just surviving. When I was out there, surrounded by them, even though I knew I was going to die, I felt more alive than I have since this whole thing went down." Taron straightened up as he talked and appeared on the verge of rising before he was interrupted.

"So you are saying you wished we left you to die?" Hector snapped, his patience wearing thin.

Taron gave a choked laugh as he settled back down.

"No, I'm grateful to you for that. I'm just saying that this allowed me to see the bigger picture. We don't have to live like this. We can go out there, fight back, and rebuild." Taron's eyes gleamed from behind the layer of gore.

"I don't understand," Henry spoke, as he saw Vanessa begin to stir on the bed deeper in the shelter. "We are together here, we are a family. There is nothing that can tear us apart."

"Mommy," James called out.

"That's all true, but there are so many people out there, and those things. It's not radiation, or mutants. We are not fighting terrorists with hidden bombs and conspiracies. We are talking about fighting the dead. They are slow and brainless. Together, we … the survivors … we can fight back. We don't need to fear them." Taron rose to his feet as if his defiance would help sway their minds.

James slid from his father's lap and moved toward his mother, who was walking groggily toward the table.

Henry called him back, Hector jumped up from the table, and Taron turned around, just as Vanessa sank her teeth into Taron's throat, tearing away a thick chunk of flesh. The sounds of her teeth puncturing his skin were no different than if she were eating a tomato from their garden back home.

Taron tried to scream, but all that came out was a thick gout of dark crimson blood. It spewed from the hole in his neck like water from the blowhole of a surfacing whale. The spray covered Vanessa, who stood chewing the mouthful of wet meat, while juices dribbled from the corners of her mouth.

Henry felt his world slow down, as everything around him lost focus. Taron fell to the floor, revealing Vanessa like a falling curtain on a matchmaking gameshow.

Hector lunged forward but slipped in the spreading pool of blood that covered the floor, and could only watch on as Vanessa swallowed her mouthful of meat and grabbed at James, whose momentum toward the creature that used to be his mother, was too great to be reversed.

Henry screamed as fear consumed him, and as his world fell to black, the last thing he heard was his son screaming.

THE END

CHECK OUT OTHER GREAT ZOMBIE NOVELS

Z BURBIA
by Jake Bible

Whispering Pines is a classic, quiet, private American subdivision on the edge of Asheville, NC, set in the pristine Blue Ridge Mountains. Which is good since the zombie apocalypse has come to Western North Carolina and really put suburban living to the test!

Surrounded by a sea of the undead, the residents of Whispering Pines have adapted their bucolic life of block parties to scavenging parties, common area groundskeeping to immediate area warfare, neighborhood beautification to neighborhood fortification.

But, even in the best of times, suburban living has its ups and downs what with nosy neighbors, a strict Home Owners' Association, and a property management company that believes the words "strict interpretation" are holy words when applied to the HOA covenants. Now with the zombie apocalypse upon them even those innocuous, daily irritations quickly become dramatic struggles for personal identity, family security, and straight up survival.

ZOMBIE RULES
by David Achord

Zach Gunderson's life sucked and then the zombie apocalypse began.

Rick, an aging Vietnam veteran, alcoholic, and prepper, convinces Zach that the apocalypse is on the horizon. The two of them take refuge at a remote farm. As the zombie plague rages, they face a terrifying fight for survival.

They soon learn however that the walking dead are not the only monsters.

CHECK OUT OTHER GREAT ZOMBIE NOVELS

DEAD ASCENT
by Jason McPhearson

The dead have risen and they are hungry...

Grizzled war veteran turned game warden, Brayden James and a small group of survivors, fight their way through the rugged wilderness of southern Appalachia to an isolated cabin in the hope of finding sanctuary. Every terrifying step they make they are stalked by a growing mass of staggering corpses, and a raging forest fire, set by the government in hopes of containing the virus.

As all logical routes off the mountain are cut off from them, they seek the higher ground, but they soon realize there is little hope of escape when the dead walk and the world burns.

CHAOS THEORY
by Rich Restucci

The world has fallen to a relentless enemy beyond reason or mercy. With no remorse they rend the planet with tooth and nail.

One man stands against the scourge of death that consumes all.

Teamed with a genius survivalist and a teenage girl, he must flee the teeming dead, the evils of humans left unchecked, and those that would seek to use him. His best weapon to stave off the horrors of this new world? His wit.

CHECK OUT OTHER GREAT ZOMBIE NOVELS

900 MILES
by S. Johnathan Davis

John is a killer, but that wasn't his day job before the Apocalypse.

In a harrowing 900 mile race against time to get to his wife just as the dead begin to rise, John, a business man trapped in New York, soon learns that the zombies are the least of his worries, as he sees first-hand the horror of what man is capable of with no rules, no consequences and death at every turn.

Teaming up with an ex-army pilot named Kyle, they escape New York only to stumble across a man who says that he has the key to a rumored underground stronghold called Avalon..... Will they find safety? Will they make it to Johns wife before it's too late?

Get ready to follow John and Kyle in this fast paced thriller that mixes zombie horror with gladiator style arena action!

WHITE FLAG OF THE DEAD
by Joseph Talluto

Millions died when the Enillo Virus swept the earth. Millions more were lost when the victims of the plague refused to stay dead, instead rising to slaughter and feed on those left alive. For survivors like John Talon and his son Jake, they are faced with a choice: Do they submit to the dead, raising the white flag of surrender? Or do they find the will to fight, to try and hang on to the last shreds or humanity?

www.ingramcontent.com/pod-product-compliance
Lightning Source LLC
Chambersburg PA
CBHW051954170626
46808CB00007B/2620